"What are you doing?"

"Leaving a going-away gift for your boss." Bolan held up the thermite grenades so the mobster could see. "It's about to get hot in there."

"You can't destroy everything! You know how much that merchandise is worth?"

"More than pocket change, but you're going out of business, so it won't make much difference."

Bolan went back inside the warehouse. He planted the thermite grenades in among the stacked cartons, pulled the pins and made a quick exit. As the Executioner stepped outside, he heard the hiss of the grenades activating. Stark light filled the warehouse as the thermite compound began to burn. By the time the process was completed there wouldn't be much left.

Bolan opened the car door and tossed a cell phone onto the mobster's lap.

"Now you can call home. Tell Tsvetanov we win round one."

MACK BOLAN ®
The Executioner

THE EXECUTIONER

DON PENDLETON'S

MAXIMUM CHAOS

A GOLD EAGLE BOOK FROM

WORLDWIDE®

TORONTO • NEW YORK • LONDON
AMSTERDAM • PARIS • SYDNEY • HAMBURG
STOCKHOLM • ATHENS • TOKYO • MILAN
MADRID • WARSAW • BUDAPEST • AUCKLAND

If you purchased this book without a cover you should be aware that this book is stolen property. It was reported as "unsold and destroyed" to the publisher, and neither the author nor the publisher has received any payment for this "stripped book."

Recycling programs
for this product may
not exist in your area.

First edition October 2014

ISBN-13: 978-0-373-64431-5

Special thanks and acknowledgment to
Mike Linaker for his contribution to this work.

MAXIMUM CHAOS

Copyright © 2014 by Worldwide Library

All rights reserved. Except for use in any review, the
reproduction or utilization of this work in whole or in part
in any form by any electronic, mechanical or other means,
now known or hereafter invented, including xerography,
photocopying and recording, or in any information storage
or retrieval system, is forbidden without the written permission
of the publisher, Worldwide Library, 225 Duncan Mill Road,
Don Mills, Ontario M3B 3K9, Canada.

This is a work of fiction. Names, characters, places and incidents are
either the product of the author's imagination or are used fictitiously,
and any resemblance to actual persons, living or dead, business
establishments, events or locales is entirely coincidental.

® and TM are trademarks of the publisher. Trademarks indicated
with ® are registered in the United States Patent and Trademark
Office, the Canadian Intellectual Property Office and in other countries.

Printed in U.S.A.

The battlefield is a scene of constant chaos. The winner will be the one who controls that chaos, both his own and the enemy's.

—Napoleon Bonaparte

The forces of chaos cannot be controlled, not by any man. But chaos can be fought, and I will continue to fight as long as innocent lives are on the line.

—Mack Bolan

THE
MACK BOLAN
LEGEND

Nothing less than a war could have fashioned the destiny of the man called Mack Bolan. Bolan earned the Executioner title in the jungle hell of Vietnam.

But this soldier also wore another name—Sergeant Mercy. He was so tagged because of the compassion he showed to wounded comrades-in-arms and Vietnamese civilians.

Mack Bolan's second tour of duty ended prematurely when he was given emergency leave to return home and bury his family, victims of the Mob. Then he declared a one-man war against the Mafia.

He confronted the Families head-on from coast to coast, and soon a hope of victory began to appear. But Bolan had broken society's every rule. That same society started gunning for this elusive warrior—to no avail.

So Bolan was offered amnesty to work within the system against terrorism. This time, as an employee of Uncle Sam, Bolan became Colonel John Phoenix. With a command center at Stony Man Farm in Virginia, he and his new allies—Able Team and Phoenix Force—waged relentless war on a new adversary: the KGB.

But when his one true love, April Rose, died at the hands of the Soviet terror machine, Bolan severed all ties with Establishment authority.

Now, after a lengthy lone-wolf struggle and much soul-searching, the Executioner has agreed to enter an "arm's-length" alliance with his government once more, reserving the right to pursue personal missions in his Everlasting War.

1

The man's voice had been electronically altered, giving it a harsh metallic sound.

"Listen without interruption, Mr. Mason. By now you will realize your daughter has been taken. At this moment in time, she is unharmed. Whether she stays that way is entirely up to you. To ensure the safe return of young Abigail, you must negotiate the release of Leopold Marchinski. You have one week to carry out this request. If Marchinski is not a free man at midnight on the final day, your daughter will die. You may speak now. Do you have questions?"

Mason's throat had all but seized up. He fought back the utter panic that threatened to render him dumb and forced himself to take control of his emotions and deal with the caller by asserting a degree of calm.

"You took my child, damn you. Wasn't that enough? Why kill Nancy?"

"Yes, the fair Miss Cleland. She put up such a struggle defending your daughter. As to her death…it demonstrates that we are in earnest. If you fail to have Marchinski released on the due date, your daughter dies. Imagine little Abby being killed in a similar manner to Nancy Cleland. Our people, though crude, are effective. Bear that in mind."

"Tell me my daughter is…"

"I hope you were not about to say safe. Abigail is not in a safe environment. That is the whole reason for this call."

Mason gathered his thoughts before he spoke.

"For all I know, she may already be dead. Unless you prove she's alive I have no reason to carry on this conversation. Show me proof before we go any further."

"I can see why you are a successful negotiator, Mason."

"Then negotiate this," Mason snapped, feeling sweat pop out across his face as he pushed the boundaries. "Abby is all you have to bargain with. So prove to me she's still alive or I put this phone down now. If you expect me to play your sick game I'll need real-time proof, regularly, that she's alive."

"And if I refuse? What then?"

"Then Marchinski takes whatever comes to him and I lose my daughter. Simple enough for you to understand."

"A bluff."

"You think so? Try me. I'm in a corner. I have to do whatever it takes."

The silence hurt. Mason wondered whether he had overplayed his hand. But he had no choice.

"Contact will be made, so keep your cell handy. Just remember we have the girl. Two hours from now, you'll have your proof."

"Wait," Mason said, "how do you expect me to free Marchinski? He's in confinement. On twenty-four-hour watch. I can't simply walk in and lead him out by the hand."

"You're a man of great influence in the justice system. Make it happen."

"It's impossible."

"Then your daughter will die in one week. The math is simple. No Marchinski—no Abigail." A pause, then, "And please don't involve the authorities. No police. No FBI. No one. Believe me when I say we have connections. Any attempt to involve assistance will mean Abigail suffers. If you don't believe me, go ahead and make a call. Abigail will die before anyone gets near us. Please do not make the mistake of treating me like a fool. You saw what happened to Nancy. Keep that image in your mind. Think about your daughter."

"How can I—"

"Make contact? You can't, but I can call you at any time. Your cell. Your house phone. We can listen to any call you make."

Mason wasn't sure that was a genuine threat. On the other hand, he couldn't afford to take the chance.

"I need time."

"I can hear your mind working, Mason. How can I get around this? How do I beat it? A word of advice—do not even try. Concentrate on freeing Marchinski. That is the most important thing in your life right now. That and keeping your daughter alive. Seven days, Mason."

The call ended.

A simple click, and Mason was left holding a silent phone.

HE SAT WITH the dead phone in his hand, staring out the living-room window, seeing nothing as he replayed the conversation over and over.

The man was not fooling. When Mason had driven to the lodge and walked inside, he'd found the butchered body of the young woman he employed to look after Abby.

Nancy Cleland had been 25 years old, a raven-haired British woman who'd worked for Mason for three years. Her body had been reduced to a bloody mass of torn and slashed flesh. Every finger on her hands had been broken and twisted out of shape. Someone had killed her in a terrible way—something Mason could never have imagined in his worst nightmare. The plastic sheet she lay on was pooled with blood.

Mason couldn't remember how long he'd stood there—his back against the door, his gaze fixed on the dead woman. When the spell broke, he went from room to room, calling out Abby's name. He searched the entire lodge. Abby was not there. Tears ran down his face as he went to call the police. That was when he saw an envelope taped to the phone.

Inside the envelope were two items.

The first was a Polaroid photo of his daughter, taken in the same room where Nancy's body now lay. In the picture, Abby was sitting in one of the chairs, staring at the camera. Her face was pale and her eyes were wide with shock.

The second item was a folded sheet of paper. When Mason unfolded it, he read the handwritten note—

We have Abby. If you tell anyone, she will die. Secure the lodge, go home and wait for a call. Now.

MASON HAD NEVER felt this helpless. He was a federal prosecutor with the power of the legal machine at his fingertips. Now he was on his own. As much as he needed his daughter back alive and well, he understood his responsibility to the law.

Leopold Marchinski was the head of a criminal organization. He sentenced men to death as easily as ordering a pizza. His criminal empire, spread across the eastern seaboard, was involved in countless illegal enterprises. Nothing was too depraved if it brought in money.

Marchinski had the best legal protection available. He was an old-time hoodlum writ large, reveling in his status as an untouchable. The man seemed to have everyone in his pocket—from lowly street cops to members of the judiciary.

For once, Marchinski had stepped over the line. He'd been caught on camera personally eliminating an employee. It was an error brought on by the man's arrogance—his contempt for the law—and it had marked him down for retribution through due process.

Larry Mason had inherited the case, and he was determined to see Marchinski sentenced and imprisoned. Mason had been after the mobster for a long time. He'd weathered the threats and the intimidation up to this moment.

Now he faced the one thing he couldn't accept—the death of his daughter. Abigail, the bright star in his life. Mason's wife had died of cancer two years after the child was born. Abby was all he had left. She was nine years old, a beautiful girl who'd inherited her mother's looks and intelligence. Everything Mason did was for his daughter.

He was trapped in an impossible position.

Did he sacrifice his child by refusing to bend to Marchinski's demands?

Or go against everything he stood for and use his position and power to attempt the release of a vicious, unrepentant killer?

Mason had always prided himself on being able to

master any situation. But he had no idea how to deal with this nightmare.

He left the house, climbed into his car and drove. The use of his landline and even his cell phone was out of the question. So he headed to the closest shopping center. Mason parked and walked into the mall, taking an escalator to the uppermost floor, where a bank of pay phones was adjacent to the food court. He dialed a number he hadn't called for some time and waited.

"Hal, it's Larry. I need your help. Can we meet? The place where we told you Heather was pregnant. That's right. An hour? See you then."

Washington, D.C.

THE PARK WAS nearly deserted. A sudden rainstorm had cleared the wide swathes of grass and trees. Mason slipped on a long waterproof coat and jammed an old ball cap over his hair. As he crossed the lot, he picked out his friend's broad-shouldered form waiting under the branches of the massive oak. Mason crossed the grass and came face-to-face with his old friend.

"Larry, what's this all about?" Hal Brognola asked.

Struggling to keep his emotions under control, Mason explained what had happened. Brognola listened, his face betraying his own shock at hearing that Abby—his goddaughter—had been kidnapped. When Mason finished, Brognola was silent for long moments.

Mason's cell rang. He glanced at his watch and saw the two hours were up. His tormentors were nothing if not punctual.

"Hal, don't speak. We need to keep this silent."

Brognola nodded. Mason pressed a key and took the call.

The screen brightened into a video of Mason's daughter, holding up a newspaper. The print was clear, and Mason could read the current date beside the paper's headline. Abigail's eyes were wide in agitation as she stared directly at the camera. Behind the child was a blank wall.

The electronic voice said, "Tomorrow morning, you'll get the same proof. Just remember, time is running out."

The image jerked briefly and the screen went blank. Mason stared at it for a while, saying nothing.

"Okay," Brognola said. "We keep this between ourselves. No agency involvement. Marchinski might have contacts within the law community."

"How do we handle it, Hal? I have seven days to turn Marchinski loose. If I don't, Abby dies. I know the man. He'll do it just to prove a point, even if he doesn't get out. I want her back, but how can I justify freeing an animal like Marchinski?"

Brognola cleared his throat. "Larry, do you trust me?"

"Hell, yes. There's no question. Why do you think I came to you, Hal?"

"Then turn around and go home. Go to work in the morning as you normally do. For now, we play Marchinski's game. Let them believe you're working on his release. Lie through your teeth if you have to. Just keep him dangling."

MASON FELT THE hours slipping away. The days counting down to the death of his daughter.

He didn't regret contacting Hal Brognola. The man was more than just a friend. They had known each other for over fifteen years. Brognola breathed the concepts of law and justice. He was a dependable, smart man, whom Mason trusted without a shadow of a doubt.

Even so, Mason couldn't help wondering if this was out of Hal Brognola's scope.

He returned to his house and switched on his laptop, bringing up the extensive file on Marchinski. He wasn't sure what he was looking for, whether any of the pages of information could suggest some way he could outmaneuver the man.

After an hour, he pushed to his feet and went to the kitchen. He forced himself to prepare a pot of coffee, the smell of freshly ground beans failing to work their usual magic. Mason waited while the coffee percolated, and when it was ready he filled a mug and stood over it, distracted by the thoughts churning through his mind.

Who was he kidding?

This wasn't going to work. Not even Hal Brognola could return Abby unhurt.

"Is there enough in that pot for one more mug?"

The voice, coming from behind him, was strong and firm, and it had a quality Mason found uplifting.

He turned and saw the man standing a few feet behind him. Relaxed. Confident.

Mack Bolan, aka the Executioner, had just joined the fight.

2

"Hal told me about your problem," the stranger said. "Let's see if we can figure out a solution."

Mason found himself filling a second mug and sliding it across the kitchen counter.

"Matt Cooper," the man said by way of introduction.

He was tall, Mason saw. Over six feet and dark-haired. Cooper's eyes were an intense shade of blue, and he studied Mason with an unflinching gaze. He was well built, but there was a relaxed grace to his movements. Dressed in black, Cooper wore a thin leather jacket, unzipped, so that when he turned Mason spotted the shoulder-holstered auto pistol.

"I was told not to involve any…"

"You asked Hal for help. You told him not to bring in any official agencies."

"You're not a cop? FBI?"

Bolan smiled. "Only three people are in on this. You, Hal and me."

"You work for Hal?" Mason asked.

"I work with Hal, but you won't find my name on any official databases, and I don't carry a badge."

Mason sat back on one of the kitchen stools.

"You must figure I'm ungrateful. Suspicious."

"Larry, I'd be worried if you weren't."

"The guy who called threatened to murder Abby if I brought in outside help."

"He wants you so scared you'll do everything he demands."

"Like releasing Marchinski?" Mason shook his head. "His people overestimate my influence. It isn't in my power."

"Then we need to get your daughter back before the deadline."

"How?"

"That's my part of the deal. Yours is to stall Marchinski's people. They have to believe you're attempting to free him. I don't care how you do it, but keep them believing. If Marchinski has people in the system, we have to give them something to pass back to the organization."

Mason nodded. "I'll work something out." He stared at Bolan. "Can we do this, Mr. Cooper?"

"To get Abby back we have to. And it's Matt," he said. "Hal told me how you forced the caller into updating you about Abby. That was a good move. It pushes the responsibility back into their hands. They have to keep Abby alive and keep proving it to you."

"I had no other ideas on how to handle things."

"You did great. Now it's my turn to push them."

"Do I need to know how you're going to do it?"

Bolan drained his mug of coffee. "Better you don't."

"I understand."

"Whatever happens, the Marchinski organization is going to have a bad week. They chose the rules for this game, so they can take the hits."

The implication behind Bolan's words was not lost on Larry Mason. But these were the men who'd killed Nancy Cleland and kidnapped his daughter.

"Is there anything I can do to help? I can't even give you an idea of who this caller is. The voice was altered."

"Get in touch with Hal. Tell him I suggested we try tracing this caller the next time he makes contact." Bolan slipped a cell phone from his pocket and handed it to Mason. "This is a prepaid burner. My number and Hal's are already logged in. Nothing else. You need to tell me something or ask a question, I'm available anytime. If Hal calls it'll be on this cell, as well. No one else will be able to get to you on this phone."

Mason took the cell. "How do I say thank you?"

"When I see Abby back in your arms, that'll be thanks enough."

There was a framed photograph on the kitchen counter. A bright-eyed and attractive child smiling at the camera.

"Is that Abby?"

Mason nodded. "It was taken only a few weeks ago at a friend's birthday party. Do you need it?"

"No. I'll recognize her now."

"Nine years old and she's smarter than me sometimes. A week ago she won her Judo upgrade. Hal told you about Nancy, I guess? Abby's nanny. I saw what they did to her, so I understand the kind of people we're dealing with. I realize the danger my daughter is in."

"Then you know how I need to handle this."

Bolan turned and walked out of the kitchen, leaving the house the same way he'd entered, through the rear door and across the garden. Mason didn't attempt to follow. For the first time since the phone call from Abby's kidnapper, he felt there might be a chance he would get her back alive and well.

BOLAN HEADED TOWARD his Chevy Suburban. There was no sign of anyone trailing him.

Marchinski's people were not amateurs. His organization comprised violent, greedy individuals who ruled by fear. The deal they had set up with Mason was delicate, and they would want to make sure he was following the rules. Even so, keeping a close watch on Mason would be difficult for the mobsters. His neighborhood was upmarket, the houses secure. There would be regular security patrols and the neighbors would not tolerate unknown vehicles being parked in clear sight or strangers wandering by.

Reaching his vehicle—which was parked on a feeder road at the far side of the residential estate—he keyed the lock release and slid behind the wheel. After hitting the start button, he wheeled the car away from the curb. Bolan drove until he spotted the shopping mall he'd seen on his way in. He swung into the parking lot and stopped the car. Bolan took out his cell and tapped in the speed-dial number for Brognola. It only took a brief time for the secure connection to be made, and Hal Brognola picked up.

"Striker," Brognola said. "What do you think?"

"Mason is a good man. He doesn't deserve this."

"The real question is can we help him? We don't have a great deal to go on here."

"I've set him up with a clean cell, and I told him to contact you. Get Bear to fix it so any calls that go to his home or regular cell can be traced. We might get lucky and record a voice for analysis."

Aaron "the Bear" Kurtzman was head of the cybernetics team at Stony Man Farm. If anyone could track down Abby's kidnapper, it would be Kurtzman.

"And in the meantime?"

"In the meantime, I start to shake the organization's tree. See what drops out of the branches. Marchinski and his brother, Gregor, want to play down and dirty. That suits me fine. Snatching that child has painted a target on every man who takes Marchinski's money."

"Should we expect some damage here?"

"Only for the organization. I need up-to-date information on the Marchinski crew—backgrounds, establishments and business rivals. I'm going to pay them all a visit."

"All in hand," Brognola said, and he gave Bolan a verbal rundown on Marchinski's crime family.

Nothing was below the Marchinskis. Drugs. Slavery. Car theft. They were involved in the flesh trade, from street girls to expensive brothels. Then there were Marchinski's suspected connections in law enforcement. The informers. The judges he had on his payroll.

Marchinski's lawyer—Jason Keppler—handled all aspects of the Marchinski business consortium. Keppler was a slick operator who kept his client and his business in the clear. Keppler's law firm, with its dedicated team of like-minded legal experts, made sure the law didn't trouble their clients.

Until the moment Leo Marchinski made his fatal error. Executing one of his own, to prove his strength. Marchinski had been caught on not one, but two, cameras. The overwhelming evidence had fallen into police hands, and despite attempts to destroy it, the recordings had been secured. Mason had seen the tapes and found himself with enough proof to have Marchinski arrested and indicted. Not even Jason Keppler had been able to argue away the graphic images. There was no doubt who had pulled the trigger. Leo Marchinski was held in jail and charged with first-degree murder.

If Bolan was going to make sure the mobster stayed behind bars, he needed a way to get to the Marchinskis—something he could use to rattle their cage. He wanted to give them something to focus on apart from their scheme to free Leo. To do that, Bolan needed information on their setup, their bases.

It didn't take him long to find a solution to that problem.

3

Trenton, New Jersey

Harry Jigs had no love for either Leopold Marchinski or his rival, Dragomir Tsvetanov. The fifty-six-year-old small-time hustler was no saint, but he considered himself at least human compared to the larger crime syndicates.

The sparring organizations had spoiled life for a number of lesser criminals as they gathered up the city districts. Low-level outfits either sold out to the bigger groups or were swept aside. A number of Jigs's friends, working similar low-key deals, had tried to fight back, but they'd failed, and in some instances forfeited their lives. People disappeared. Sometimes their bodies turned up on vacant lots or were found floating in the water. The message eventually sank in and resistance fell to the wayside.

Jigs had seen the writing on the wall so he'd left the game. He'd salted away enough money to live above the breadline. He had no family to support and he didn't own a car or a house—he lived in the same cramped apartment he'd rented for years. Jigs was a survivor. These days, he added to his savings by peddling information. Nothing grand. Just small stuff he picked up from keeping his eyes and ears open and his mouth shut.

One of Jigs's best customers was a man named Matt Cooper. Jigs knew very little about the man, apart from his direct and unapologetic manner. Cooper was honest and without any kind of hidden agenda. He might have been a cop, or even some kind of Federal operative. Whatever his profession, Cooper paid well for information.

And Jigs was in desperate need of a payday. Sitting in his favorite coffee shop, Jigs perched stiffly on the bench seat, facing the window. Scanning the sidewalk outside, Jigs saw nothing to alarm him. Just people passing by, going about their business. It seemed like an ordinary day. Jigs hoped it stayed that way.

He spotted Cooper as the man walked past the window and turned in at the door. Cooper stopped at the counter to order a drink, then joined Jigs at his table, slipping onto the bench alongside him.

"Been a while, Mr. Cooper," Jigs said. His hand trembled slightly until he realized and clenched his fingers.

Matt Cooper stared out the window. The first drops of rain hit the glass and slid down.

"Harry, I remember you had trouble a few years back with Marchinski and Tsvetanov. You still want a chance to get back at them?"

Jigs had time to consider the question as Cooper's coffee was brought to the table. He waited until the server had walked away before he spoke.

"Now that's a hell of a way to start a conversation."

"I could ask how you are or talk about the weather, if that's what you want."

Jigs gave a short chuckle. "Or you could shoot straight to the point."

"I need a way to get at Marchinski's mob—through Tsvetanov, if possible."

Jigs listened, his face immobile as he absorbed Cooper's words. Almost from the word *go,* he was interested. Anything that might aggravate the organizations was good in Jigs's book.

"This liable to lead back to me?" he asked. "You know what those assholes are like."

"I just need you to point me in the right direction, Harry. I'm looking for locations where they might have an operation going on, a few names I can zero in on. No one needs to know where my information came from."

Jigs smiled.

He slid a ballpoint pen from his pocket and began to write, filling a paper napkin with information and talking as he wrote. Once he was finished, Jigs drained his coffee and watched Cooper pick up the napkin and glance at it before tucking it away in his pocket.

"Covers both sides," Jigs said. "Hit any of those locations and you hurt them where it matters."

"Thanks, Harry. That's all I need." Cooper drew a folded envelope from his pocket and passed it to the man under the table. "Buy yourself a steak dinner."

From the thickness of the envelope, Jigs realized he'd be able to buy himself a plentiful supply of steaks and a private table to go with them.

Cooper stood, dropping a ten-dollar bill on the table. "For the coffee," he said. "You watch your back."

"I'll do some more checking," Jigs said. "See what else I can dig up."

"No risks, Harry. Just take it easy," Bolan said.

"There's a cell number on the inside of the envelope. You can contact me if anything comes up."

"Okay."

"Remember what I said. Don't go out on a limb."

"You got it," Jigs said.

Cooper walked out of the coffee shop, turning up his collar against the rain as he stepped out onto the street. A moment later he was gone. And Jigs was on his own once again.

MACK BOLAN MADE his way back to his SUV. He sat for a moment, listening to the rain drum on the roof, his mind working as he selected one of the locations on Jigs's napkin. He took out his cell and called Stony Man Farm, greeting Barbara Price when she answered. He gave her the information from Jigs and asked for details on the first location. He also asked for photo ID of organization members, if possible.

"Have Bear check police files. They might not have been convicted but I'm pretty sure most of the perps have been pulled in over the years, so there'll be mug shots."

"I'll have everything downloaded to your cell."

"That's good," Bolan said. He read out the rest of the information Jigs had given him. "Same with these."

"You planning a vacation?" Price asked.

"No. Just working on targets."

Price didn't reply instantly. "Be safe, Striker. There are people here who care about you."

"That works both ways," Bolan said before ending the call.

As he fired up the SUV, he heard his phone ping. That would be his first information feed from Stony

Man. He checked the download, then drove to the motel he was using as a temporary base.

Bolan parked outside his unit, grabbed a large carryall from the SUV and took it inside. He dropped the bag onto the bed and unzipped it. Along with some changes of clothing, Bolan had brought a selection of weapons to add to the Beretta 93R he was already wearing. He checked his supplies then crossed the room to make some coffee.

It was the same in a thousand motels across the country—an electric kettle, a couple of mugs and a supply of sachets holding coffee, tea and small cartons of sterilized milk. Bolan wasn't in the mood to find a diner, but he needed some caffeine and the comparative privacy of the anonymous room. He filled the kettle and set it to boil.

His cell pinged again. Bolan sat on the edge of the bed and scanned the information Aaron Kurtzman and the Stony Man cyber team had compiled.

Marchinski and Tsvetanov were both hotheaded thugs with the delusion they were invincible. They ran their organizations along predictable lines—working in the basest criminal theaters and using violence, intimidation and bribery. As he moved down the list, Bolan realized the organizations operated in every possible illegal trade: drugs, prostitution, theft, pornography and human trafficking.

Bolan's water had boiled, so he made a quick mug of coffee and kept going through the data. Jigs had supplied the bare bones and Kurtzman had fleshed out all the details, giving Bolan enough ammunition to bring Executioner fury down on the crime syndicates.

Bolan's main concern was retrieving Abby Mason

alive and well, but his forays against Marchinski and Tsvetanov would add a sweetener to his strikes.

Disrupting the lives of Marchinski and Tsvetanov would take the spotlight off Abby—even if it was only for a short time—and that breather would allow Bolan to work his way through the organizations, removing some of their top men while he found out where the girl was being held.

4

Trenton, New Jersey

Harry Jigs's information was proving out.

The Tsvetanov warehouse was one of many in an old industrial park on the fringes of Trenton. It was late afternoon by the time Bolan cruised through the worn-down area, taking in the shabby buildings and storage facilities. A couple of expensive cars were parked alongside one storage area; they were high-end models that looked out of place behind a sagging wire fence.

Bolan rounded the west side of the yard—easing the SUV along a narrow service road—and parked at the far end, angling the vehicle so he'd have an easy exit. Kurtzman had sent an aerial view of the neighborhood, allowing Bolan to check out available escape routes.

The Executioner wore black clothing complemented by a pair of grip-soled ankle boots. Beneath his soft leather jacket he carried the suppressed Beretta 93R with an extended magazine for extra firepower. He had a keen-bladed lock knife in one of the pockets of the jacket.

The soldier didn't yet know the strength of his enemy. Nor did he have any idea of their abilities— not the most advisable way of walking into the enemy camp. But Bolan was running out of time, and the life of a child was at stake—he had no choice but to take a calculated risk.

Bolan locked the Suburban and moved to the weak section of fence that he'd spotted on approach. The sagging wire allowed him to slip through easily. Bolan moved quickly to press up against the blank end wall of the warehouse. He unleathered the 93R, removing the machine pistol from under his jacket and easing the selector to single shot.

After scanning the area, Bolan chose to make his way around to the rear; the ground was strewn with debris, and there was nothing beyond the fence but a steep, weed-choked bank. Stepping carefully to avoid kicking any loose debris, Bolan moved across the face of the building until he reached a service door that stood partway open. He could hear muted voices beyond the door, telling him someone was home.

Bolan slipped through the door and crouched in the shadows. The interior was gloomy, the medium-sized storage building half-full of stacked cardboard cartons. Along the wall to Bolan's right was a partitioned office with three men inside. As Bolan worked his way through the stacked cartons, the voices increased in volume and the men waved their arms through the coils of cigarette smoke floating around their heads.

One of the men in the office turned and snatched open the door. He leaned out and yelled at a fourth man.

"Hey, shithead, go and secure that back door. It's time we moved…"

The office door slammed shut.

A lean figure emerged from the shadows just beyond where Bolan crouched. The guy was armed with an SMG and had an auto pistol jammed into his belt. He was muttering to himself as he headed toward the door.

Bolan waited until the last possible moment before rising from cover. He slammed the hard edge of his left hand into the gunman's throat just beneath his jaw. The blow crunched home. The man dropped his SMG, clutching his throat with both hands, eyes staring wildly. He started to make choking sounds as he tried—and failed—to suck air into his crushed windpipe. The man dropped to his knees as Bolan stepped around him and opened one of the cartons.

Bolan was not surprised to find the carton stacked with porn DVDs. He checked a few of the cases and found that it was material of the worst kind. Bolan looked at the rows of cartons and envisaged the total number of DVDs. According to Harry Jigs, the Tsvetanov organization was engaged in this sordid trade just as Marchinski was—both mobs appeared to be working the converging markets.

Bolan failed to suppress a grin when he realized the potential here. He could play one group against the other. When Bolan checked other cartons, he found plastic bags full of white powder; Bolan split one of the bags and checked the contents; he dipped a finger in the powder and tasted it—cocaine. Bolan spit out the trace.

Bolan snatched up the fallen gunman's SMG and checked the magazine; the weapon was an Uzi chambered for 9 mm Parabellum. The Israeli weapon had been around for a long time, and Mack Bolan was extremely familiar with it. The solid design of the weapon, with its blowback operation, had delivered Executioner justice to many of Bolan's enemies.

His mind lingered briefly on the origin of the name Parabellum. Taken from the Latin Si Vis Pacem Para

Bellum—If you seek peace, prepare for war—the phrase was close to Bolan's heart. It was something he understood and practiced.

Bolan sheathed the Beretta and headed for the office. The argument was still raging, and now that he was closer, Bolan realized the men were speaking in Russian. He had a reasonable grasp of the language and made out they were in a dispute over who was responsible for the final distribution of the goods. The confusion suited Bolan. The men would be distracted, and that gave him the advantage.

He moved along the length of the office, ducking briefly until he cleared the window then rising to his full height as he reached the door. Bolan slammed his boot against the flimsy door and it crashed open against the inside wall, the glass panel shattering.

Three startled figures spun around to face the intruder, hands sliding under their coats to grasp holstered weapons.

"Who the hell are you?" one guy snapped in English.

"Not good news," Bolan said. "Leave the guns alone."

"Screw you," the guy yelled, drawing his auto pistol.

Bolan's finger stroked the Uzi's trigger and laid a burst that hammered 9 mm slugs into the mobster's chest. The rounds blew out his back, taking flesh and spinal bone with them. He was propelled across the small office, slamming into the far wall. An expression of disbelief showed on his face as he tumbled to the floor, weapon slipping from numbed fingers. Blood oozed from the spread of holes in his torso.

Shocked as they seemed by the sudden eruption of violence, the other two still pulled their own weapons.

Bolan had no qualms about responding to the threat.

He triggered the Uzi, his burst hitting both would-be shooters at close range, 9 mm slugs ripping into them. The men were put down instantly, bodies torn and bloody.

Bolan held the Uzi on line as he gathered fallen weapons and threw them out the office door and across the warehouse. Checking the men, he found one still alive. The mobster had caught Bolan's slugs in his right side and shoulder, which were torn and bloody now, splintered bone gleaming white in the mangled flesh. The man stared up at Bolan, his eyes holding a murderous gleam.

"You won't get away with this," he said.

"I seem to be doing okay right now. I'm not lying on the floor with bullets in me. You want to reconsider that last statement?"

The man clutched at his body, sucking ragged breaths in through his mouth.

"What are you? Cop? DEA?"

"Nothing so fancy. I'm just a working stiff like you—doing my job—which today is cutting down the opposition."

The man dragged himself up so he could lean against a wooden desk. He studied Bolan's expressionless face, looking for answers.

"Opposition? What opposition? Damn it…you work for Marchinski?"

"You're a bright boy. Work it out. It's time to shorten the odds."

"Tsvetanov will kill you for this. He'll tear off your fucking head."

"Just tell him this is only the start," Bolan said. "Tell him to pull up the drawbridge and back off, or he'll get to see what else we have for him."

Bolan ran a quick search and retrieved two cell phones from the dead men. He searched the wounded guy and located his.

"Wouldn't want you calling home just yet," Bolan said.

"What else you got to do?"

"Waiting to see is where the fun comes in."

Bolan hauled the man to his feet and half dragged him outside. He pushed the mobster onto the front seat of one of the cars. From his back pocket Bolan produced plastic ties. He looped one of the ties around the guy's wrist and secured him to the steering wheel.

"Hey, you shot me. I'm hurting here."

"That so?"

Bolan pulled the lock knife from its sheath, opened the blade and methodically punctured tires on the two parked cars. Then he followed the line of the warehouse and slipped out through the fence. He opened his SUV and unzipped the heavy carryall. Bolan took out a number of thermite grenades, courtesy of Stony Man's armory, and returned to the warehouse through the deepening gloom.

"What are you doing?" the man asked as Bolan walked back into sight.

"Leaving a going-away gift for your boss." He held up the thermite grenades so the mobster could see. "It's about to get hot in there."

"You can't destroy everything! You know how much that merchandise is worth?"

"More than pocket change, but you're going out of business so it won't make much difference."

Bolan went back inside the warehouse. He planted the thermite grenades in among the stacked cartons, pulled the pins on each grenade and made a quick exit.

As the Executioner stepped outside he heard the hiss of the grenades activating. Stark light filled the warehouse as the thermite compound began to burn, igniting Tsvetanov's property. By the time the process was completed, there wouldn't be much left.

Bolan opened the car door and tossed a cell phone onto the mobster's lap.

"Now you can call home. Tell Tsvetanov we win round one."

The wounded man stared at Bolan. "I'll remember you."

Bolan's smile was predatory. "It's always nice to be remembered," he said and slammed the door.

He made his way back to his SUV. Through the grimy upper windows of the warehouse, the interior pulsed with the white glare of the thermite discharges. Bolan didn't give it a second glance. He dropped the Uzi onto the floor of the vehicle as he climbed in. Bolan started the engine and drove away slowly, without attracting any attention.

The thermite burn would consume the whole warehouse, but by the time the blaze took hold, Bolan would be heading back to his motel.

5

New York

Dragomir Tsvetanov held his temper as his man recounted what had happened at the warehouse. Holding down his rage was a supreme effort—Tsvetanov had a reputation as a wild man when it came to controlling his moods. He admitted it was a failing, though sometimes anger had its uses. A raging tirade could help keep people in check.

Today he understood the need to remain placid. He was trying to understand why Marchinski had determined that now was the time to strike out at his rival in business. The animosity between the organizations was always close to the surface, and Tsvetanov understood that it would one day erupt into violence.

But why now?

He imagined Marchinski would have enough to keep him occupied. The man was behind bars, awaiting his upcoming trial. Why would he start a war?

Tsvetanov knew Leopold Marchinski still held the reins—he ran his organization from jail. His second in command—Leo's younger brother, Gregor—would do exactly what he was told. Gregor Marchinski did not have the skill to take control of his brother's affairs. Nor did he have the courage to attempt a coup.

Maybe Marchinski was simply flexing his muscles. Showing that even if he was out of the game for the moment, he could still manage a hostile takeover. He had the manpower. The Marchinski organization employed a ruthless and experienced team. He understood the concept of dominance through superior strength. And he was never afraid to take risks. Marchinski had ambition, but he could also be greedy. Tsvetanov knew this because he held the same views and was never afraid to show his own power.

He stopped pacing the length of his office, stood and looked out the window. The tended grounds, rain soaked and shrouded in the early-morning mist, helped calm him even more. Feeling settled, albeit briefly, Dragomir—how he hated his full name; he preferred to be called Drago—faced his assistant.

"Why has Marchinski chosen this time to hit us?" he asked. "Have I missed something significant? A special date? Something I should have been aware of?"

Lexi Bulin shook his head. "Marchinski decided this was the time, I guess."

Tsvetanov stared at the man from beneath a frowning brow. Bulin was smart enough. He seldom made flippant remarks. Tsvetanov sighed.

"You really think it's as simple as that?"

"Drago, I am as confused as you. We've enjoyed a fairly amicable relationship with Marchinski. We left each other alone, yet neither trusts the other. We circle like hungry wolves. Perhaps Marchinski saw something in our organization that made him decide to strike."

"Or someone," Tsvetanov suggested.

"You think one of our people sold out?"

Tsvetanov shrugged his broad shoulders. "Perhaps an offer was too good to refuse."

Bulin waved a slim hand. He was of average height, whip-thin with a lean, almost gaunt face. He wore his dark hair down to his collar and always dressed sharply in handmade suits. His mind worked quickly.

"I would rather go with this being a preemptive strike by Marchinski. Not one of ours selling out."

"You trust them that much?"

Bulin nodded. "Yes. I don't believe they would betray you, Drago."

"Comforting to know." Tsvetanov was silent for a moment. "Is Sergei going to be all right?"

"Doctor Danton says he will live. He's going to be indisposed for a few months."

"Good. A pity about the others. Three dead. One badly injured. A full consignment destroyed. That was a great deal of money, Lexi. And we have no idea who this man was?"

"Sergei described him, but he doesn't resemble anyone we know who works for Marchinski."

"An outside triggerman? It has to be. The man knew what he was doing. He came equipped for the job and he did it. He knew the location—just walked in and took our people down. He must have been primed by Marchinski's men."

"Sergei said he was efficient. Didn't miss a thing."

Tsvetanov walked around his desk and sank into the leather swivel chair. It was a large item of furniture— the most expensive chair he'd been able to get—but Tsvetanov was not dwarfed by it. He topped the six-foot-three mark and was solidly muscular. While Bulin always dressed formally, Tsvetanov preferred expensive casual: a soft cotton, open-necked blue shirt and cream chinos, hand-worked leather loafers. Yet on his wrist a plain, fifty-dollar watch with a leather strap and a black face.

"This doesn't go unpunished, Lexi," he said, calm now. His anger had burned off and a cold, calculating mood sat in its place. "We'll get our revenge, but we'll take our time. If we go after Marchinski like a street gang, this will turn into a bloodbath. I don't want that. If it's forced on us we won't turn away, but until then, let's consider."

Bulin nodded. "What're your thoughts? Start with some short, sharp hits just to let Marchinski know we're still on the ball?"

"Exactly. But first get some of our boys on the streets. Check things out. See if there are more of Marchinski's people around than normal. Let's put our ears to the ground and listen. Someone has to know something."

"I'll get some of the guys to spread some cash around. See what the snitches have picked up."

Tsvetanov nodded. "I'll leave that in your hands, Lexi. In the meantime, I need to talk to Dushka. Have a replacement consignment organized and find a new place to store it."

Bulin made for the door.

"Have the kitchen send in some breakfast," Tsvetanov called.

The door closed behind Bulin, leaving Tsvetanov alone in the silent office. He sat for a moment, considering. It had been a bad start to the day, but he needed to look ahead. In the long run, Marchinski may have done him a favor. The confrontation that had been simmering in the background looked as if it was about to erupt. That would mean a busy time ahead. Leopold Marchinski, lounging in his jail cell while his mob ran around doing his bidding, was about to have another problem heaped on his shoulders.

Drago Tsvetanov had built up his organization from nothing. In Moscow he'd worked for his Uncle Vassily, eventually taking over the family business. But Tsvetanov had always wanted to go to America, and ten years ago he had achieved that ambition.

Once he'd arrived, Tsvetanov organized his own team, surrounding himself with loyal and smart people. Tsvetanov expanded whenever an opening occurred—there was nothing he would not handle if it promised financial rewards. His childhood in Russia had been deprived, with little money and poor living conditions; he vowed never to let himself suffer those things again. Already wealthy when he moved to the U.S., Tsvetanov's fortunes expanded greatly. Moving into drugs and prostitution helped. And when he eased into human trafficking, he realized he'd found his place in the sun.

He surrounded himself with the best lawyers money could buy, and they worked unceasingly on his behalf. An oft-quoted saying had proved true—in America, money could buy anything.

Tsvetanov was aware his business required a ruthless attitude. There was no avoiding the fact that violence was an integral part of his life. It was needed to keep unruly people in line, and that applied to his own men as well as rivals or clients who stepped over the line. He'd never been repelled by violence. Tsvetanov himself had used force when necessary. It gave him a feeling of power…close to pleasure. That feeling of dominance over another human being was as exciting as a drug rush.

But for all his brutality, Tsvetanov had never allowed himself to be compromised…which brought his thoughts back to Leopold Marchinski. The man had slipped badly by letting himself be caught on camera as he handed out a savage beating. True, the man had attempted a clumsy robbery. Stealing from his employer and getting caught had been inexcusable. Marchinski's own mistake had been beating the man to death with a baseball bat in full view of security cameras. It had landed Marchinski in a cell, awaiting trial, and it was a given he would be convicted.

Tsvetanov was pleased to have Marchinski locked away. They were rivals. Marchinski even had a similar history to Tsvetanov; he was as close to being a clone as was possible without genetic connections. His organization operated in the same businesses, and while there were ample opportunities, the two men resented each other strongly.

It had been a shock when Bulin had informed him that the man behind the attack on the warehouse appeared to be working on behalf of Marchinski. It was a slap in the face. One he could not—would not—ignore.

With his main rival behind bars, Tsvetanov had the best chance to make a decisive strike. It needed some thought. Once started, gang war was likely to be bloody and savage.

LEOPOLD MARCHINSKI SAT patiently waiting for his lawyer to arrive. He was seated at the steel table in an interview room, his cuffed hands attached to a short chain manacle fixed to the top of the table. He wore prison garb—a bright orange jumpsuit that had the penitentiary logo printed across the back and his inmate number on the front. Marchinski hated the prison uniform. It was baggy, made of coarse material and had that insti-

tutional smell he despised. Even though he'd been in jail
for almost five months, he still couldn't get used to it.

Marchinski, though, was a man blessed with great
patience. He'd known from day one that he wasn't about
to get out of this easily, so he'd sucked it up and become
a model prisoner. He had planned to stay that way until
it suited him to change.

And now he wanted change.

He wanted out of jail.

Marchinski was no caged animal. He needed his
freedom, but he understood the position he was in. The
authorities had shown him the video of him slaughter-
ing Jake Bixby, and there was no denying he'd done
it. The image on the recording was clear and sharp.
No doubts. The camera had faithfully taped the brutal
crime—every terrible, final, bloody minute of Bixby's
life. Even his high-priced lawyer, Jason Keppler, had
told him his position was dicey. The evidence could not
be argued against. Marchinski was a career criminal
who had escaped justice for a long time. This was the
prosecution's chance to lock him up for the maximum
term, and they were not about to pass on the opportunity. Marchinski was theirs.

In retrospect, Marchinski knew he'd been foolish.
Bixby needed to be punished, to be made into an example. The mistake had been acting on a wild impulse.
Marchinski should have dealt with Bixby quietly, under
controlled circumstances, rather than attacking hog
wild. Pent-up fury had led Marchinski straight to a jail
cell.

Marchinski understood that. He was looking at a lot
of jail time—too much for someone like himself. If he
survived he'd be an old man when he came out.

He had two ways to go.

Kill himself—an option he'd seriously considered for five full seconds.

Or manipulate his way out of jail.

Getting out wouldn't be easy and once he did, he'd have to leave the U.S. and move somewhere where the authorities couldn't touch him. He could live with that. There were countries with no extradition treaties, and with his money he could live high wherever he chose.

The first step was getting out from behind the prison walls. It would have to be a well-orchestrated escape. So Marchinski had spent his empty days working on various schemes and rejecting them all until he came up with the one that had been put into action.

The kidnapping of Larry Mason's young daughter.

Mason, the man directly responsible for Marchinski's incarceration. The state's prosecutor who seemed to have made it his personal crusade to lock Marchinski away for the rest of his natural life.

Marchinski had discussed the idea with his brother over a number of visits. Gregor had gone for the idea the moment it had been explained to him. He might have blurted it out loud if Marchinski had not calmed him down, making him realize the serious nature of the discussion.

Over a couple more visits, Marchinski had detailed what the scheme would involve. Gregor had added embellishments of his own and after almost a month, they were ready to make their move.

Simple enough in theory.

Marchinski's people would kidnap Mason's daughter from the man's isolated weekend lodge and kill the child's nanny as an indication of intent. Mason would be told and given a deadline. Free Marchinski, or lose his daughter. It was a bold move, with no guarantee of success. Mason loved his child—his only link with his dead wife—but Marchinski was taking a gamble.

The first part of the plan went off without a hitch. But just as the scheme got underway, Marchinski had heard from one of his lawyers that a hard strike had taken place on Tsvetanov's turf. Three of Tsvetanov's men had been killed and one of his stash houses burned to the ground with expensive cargo inside.

For a brief time, Marchinski's attention was drawn to the incident. He couldn't figure out who had carried out the hit. There was no other crew large enough to take on Tsvetanov, and he didn't believe it was the work of any law force. That wasn't the way they operated, although it was something they dreamed about. The matter gave Marchinski something to think about when he returned to his cell; he'd ordered his lawyer to instruct his crew to check the incident out.

Later, as he slumped on his bunk, staring at the ceiling, his mind refused to move on from what had happened to Tsvetanov. Any pleasure he had initially experienced faded quickly. It was replaced with a faint but growing concern over the matter. He found he was unable to dismiss it completely. It skittered around the fringes of his thoughts—in the background but never far away. If Tsvetanov had been targeted, what had it got to do with him?

He remembered a line from an old musical show. The one they made into a movie with that bald actor— Yul Brynner.

It's a puzzlement.

6

Stony Man Farm

Bolan had Brognola on the line, and he was filling him in on his foray into Tsvetanov territory.

"You really think this is going to work, Striker?" the big Fed asked.

"Having Marchinski and Tsvetanov at each other's throats should ease the pressure on Mason a little," Bolan said. "Marchinski will be getting reports from his people about what's happened, and he'll be getting uptight because he'll figure Tsvetanov will start hitting back. He'll be focused on making sure his people are ready for anything Tsvetanov might do. That gives us a little breathing space. Just make sure Mason does his part. Make it look as if he's working on Marchinski's release."

"I hope you're right."

"So do I," Bolan said. "A nine-year-old's life depends on me working this right. Getting Marchinski and Tsvetanov to hammer each other senseless is a bonus. These bastards are due for a big fall."

"Try not to raze the town to the ground while you're doing it," Brognola said. "You have a habit of creating expensive black holes."

"That must be the other guy," Bolan said.

"Oh, yeah. The one who wears tights and a cape. So what next?"

"A nudge in Marchinski's direction," Bolan said. "Something to draw his attention."

Brognola sighed. He knew what that meant. Trouble for the Marchinski mob. News would filter back, and it would tell him the Executioner was doing what he did best.

In the past, Hal Brognola had done his best to stop Bolan. In that distant era, Bolan was considered a menace to society, an out-of-control killer wreaking his own kind of justice on the criminal fraternity. Every law-enforcement agency in America was hunting Bolan. But as time revealed Bolan was not a wild killer, but a man on a mission to eradicate the evil that was terrorizing the nation, even Brognola began to see that Bolan was a force for good.

In the end, the President had invited Bolan to come on board and work with the administration. Successive Presidents had been made aware of the covert regime occupying the Stony Man facility. The need for the Commander in Chief to have a surgical strike unit within reach had remained constant. Bolan and Stony Man had proved time and again they were needed.

A major incident at Stony Man Farm forced Bolan to assume a new role in covert operations. These days he had an arm's-length relationship with the government. He often worked with Brognola when missions for the President dovetailed with missions he would have undertaken eventually. But he still worked his own agenda and chose the targets he saw as needing his intervention. He placed himself in danger every time he stepped out of the shadows, proving to Brognola his dedication to protecting the people who were helpless against the onslaught of evil.

Now that Bolan had set his sights on the mobster, Marchinski, and by default, Tsvetanov, would be brought to their knees. Brognola had no doubts about that. Larry Mason's daughter would be the focal point in Bolan's maneuvers, but tearing down the mobs would be a consequence of that mission. Bolan would create havoc as he moved inexorably toward his goal. He could do nothing else.

Names and faces changed. Mack Bolan's ongoing war against evil never wavered.

Hal Brognola sat behind his desk at Stony Man, preparing for the havoc that would come now that the Executioner was once again on the offensive.

HARRY JIGS HAD provided Bolan with the location of one of Marchinski's businesses. Stony Man had given Bolan more specifics and the soldier was ready to make his move.

The Shake A Leg club was a cover for one of Marchinski's trafficking operations. Topless women and lap dancing, though legal, were the dubious attractions that brought in the customers. They gathered around the bar and paid for expensive drinks so they could watch the listless performances, while in the basement the club's real business operated in squalid anonymity.

The victims of the trafficking trade were kept in guarded cells. Confused and disoriented, they had no idea where they were or what awaited them. Young women snatched from their home soil and transported to America, they were watched over and ill treated if they made any kind of protest. Eventually, they would be auctioned off, sometimes singly or sometimes in batches, dependent on what individual purchasers required. The only certainty was their fate, which would be light-years away from whatever they might have been promised—likely prostitution or forced labor. It might be the twenty-first century, but for these hapless individuals, it might as well have been the Victorian era. A number of these women would be given drugs to draw their minds from the pitiful conditions they were now experiencing; it was simply a way to draw them even deeper into the darkness of their new lives.

Harry Jigs had told Bolan about the club during their meet as an extra fillip of information. He'd made it obvious that Marchinski was covered by people on the take, which was why the frequent influx of covert trafficking was overlooked. Money, Jigs said, changed hands on a number of levels, covering the operation from interference.

The Shake A Leg club stood on a slice of open ground, a less-than-glamorous building with a gaudy frontage and bare brick and plaster walls on the other three sides. The front of the club was dark at this hour, the neon display switched off. Bolan had parked a couple of streets away and made his silent way through the rain to the rear of the club. At this hour, only a few vehicles were pulled up close to the back wall.

Bolan wore a blacksuit, his 93R in a shoulder rig and a Cold Steel Tanto knife clipped to his belt. Crouching in shadow, he checked out the area and saw only two sentries; he corrected that assessment almost immediately because the men were not acting like any sentries he'd seen before.

The pair, in long leather coats, were lounging against the wall, hats pulled down across their faces. One held a stubby shotgun under his left arm, barrel pointing at the ground. His partner had both hands deep in his pockets. It was obvious neither of them were happy about being forced to keep watch in the cold and wet. That worked for Bolan; lack of enthusiasm went hand in hand with poor attention spans.

He moved past the parked cars, bringing himself close to the pair. When one of the men turned to speak to his partner, Bolan saw his opportunity. He rose from behind the vehicles, a dark shadow in the gloom. Long strides brought him up behind the sentries. Without pause, Bolan struck.

He kicked the legs out from under one man and as he went down, Bolan struck the second. A hard-edged blow from his fist crunched in beneath the startled man's jaw, smashing bone and cartilage, rendering the victim speechless. The man toppled against the wall, hugging his crippled throat and desperately trying to suck in air. As he fell away, Bolan sensed the first man pushing himself to a sitting position and trying to haul the shotgun round for a shot. Bolan didn't pause and drove his right foot out—a smashing blow that almost took the man's head off his shoulders. He went backward, a strangled cry bursting from his lips, accompanying the spurt of blood and broken teeth. The man slammed back to the wet ground, body arching in a silent protest before he jerked, then became still.

Bolan moved with practiced ease as he slipped plastic ties from a pouch on his belt and bound the wrists and feet of both downed men. He checked them both for cell phones and weapons, finding two auto pistols. Bolan unloaded the weapons, disassembled them and tossed the magazines beneath the parked cars. He unloaded the shotgun and scattered the shells then crushed the cell phones beneath his booted feet.

The door the men had been positioned near was unlocked, and Bolan unleathered the Beretta as he slipped inside. A poorly lit passage led him past a couple dark offices. Bolan moved deeper into the building. At the end of the passage he was confronted by two more doors. The first opened onto the main club area, now silent and in shadow except for a few low security lights.

Opening the second door exposed a flight of stairs leading down. He descended silently, picking up the low murmur of male voices. Reaching the bottom, Bolan rounded a brick wall and saw that the underground room stretched out into a low-ceilinged run of bar-fronted cells. Facing the cells was an open section where four men sat around a long table that allowed them to watch over the captives. Four of the cells were occupied. A haze of tobacco smoke hovered over the table.

The young women were only partially dressed and slumped on low wooden beds. There was something in the way they were acting that told Bolan they'd been given drugs to keep them quiet. They remained passive, eyes fixed on distant visions, making little effort to move.

Harry Jigs's information was proving out.

One of the seated men arched his back, flexing his arms, then glanced at his watch.

"You want to make a fresh pot of coffee, Frank? It's turning out to be a long fucking night. Sooner that transport shows up, the better."

One of the men stirred himself and stood. He was tall and lean, his head shaved. He crossed to where a smaller table held mugs and a coffeepot, picked up the pot and headed for the stairs where Bolan stood hidden by the wall.

"We should make one of those bitches do it," he complained. "All they do is sit on their asses."

"You think they're fit to even carry the coffeepot?" one of the men said, laughing. "With that shit they had pumped into them, it's a wonder they can even sit up."

The man called Frank walked to the end of the wall, turning toward the stairs.

He didn't see the black-clad figure emerge from the shadows. Blue eyes as cold as chipped ice. All he saw was a sudden movement in the gloom, then something struck him full in the face. His nose collapsed under the brutal blow as the bulk of Bolan's pistol slammed across his face. He gave a strangled cry as the excruciating pain flared, the unchecked flow of hot blood streaming from his nose, spilling down his chin and across the front of his shirt. The coffeepot slipped from his fingers. He offered no resistance as Bolan caught him by one shoulder and spun him around. Bolan's booted foot slammed against his butt, propelling Frank across the floor to slam face-first against the bars of the closest cell.

As Frank crashed against the steel bars, the other three men scrambled off their chairs, clawing for the guns they carried. As fast as they were, their actions were way behind.

Bolan had stepped into view, the Beretta already tracking in. He had set the weapon for triple-burst fire, and the repeated three-round explosions crackled with subsonic energy. Flesh yielded as Bolan's 9 mm slugs slammed home..Blood sprayed and dark fragments blew into the air as the three hardmen went down in a flurry of jerking arms and legs. Two hit the floor. The third slumped lifelessly on his chair, head back, a final gurgle of sound sliding from his throat.

Bolan holstered his pistol, pulled out a plastic tie and secured the moaning Frank. The guy was barely conscious as Bolan maneuvered him onto one of the chairs.

At one end of the cell block, a central locking lever freed the doors. Bolan swung open each cell door and helped the young women out. It was a slow task. The drugged women could barely comprehend what was happening. Only one of them seemed to fully grasp what was going on, and she summoned enough energy to gather the others together. She was the one who spotted the coats tossed carelessly on a chair. She brought them to the other women and handed them out.

"We need to go," Bolan said. "You understand?"

The woman nodded. "Yes. I understand," she said in awkward, strongly accented English.

"Take the others up the stairs. Go to the end of the passage and wait by the door for me."

Bolan turned and stood to one side of the man called Frank. He was still hunched over, blood running from his nose and a gash on his cheek. He seemed barely aware of Bolan's presence until he spoke.

"You hear me, Frank?" The man managed a nod. "When you get the chance, pass a message to your bosses. Tell them Drago Tsvetanov is moving in. The Marchinskis are finished. Tell him there's more to come—a lot more. Got that?" Bolan raised his voice. "You hear me, Frank?"

Frank nodded again. "Yeah. I hear you, and I got the message."

"Make sure it gets to home, Frank."

Bolan turned and made for the stairs, leaving behind what was left of the Marchinski crew. The four women were huddled together, waiting for him. The one who understood English turned to him.

"We can go now?"

Bolan nodded. "You're free."

Bolan led the women outside to where the parked cars stood. He opened doors and ushered them inside, out of the rain. As they slid onto the comfortable seats, Bolan leaned in and started the motor, pressing the controls that activated the interior heater.

"I have something to do and a phone call to make," he said and closed the door.

He slipped back inside the club and made a swift check of the building. Bolan was looking for Abby Mason, even though he had the feeling she wasn't at the club. He was right—the place was deserted.

Back outside, Bolan tapped the cell phone key that would connect him to Stony Man. He listened to the tone, then heard the pickup.

"It's me," he said when Barbara Price came on.

"And?" she asked.

"Strike two."

"Where?"

"One of Marchinski's less-than-wholesome establishments. Up top it's a pole-dancing emporium. In the basement it's a holding pen for trafficked women. Four of which I have waiting in a car."

"What is it with you and women in peril, Striker? Can't you just find a normal, healthy one to fill the empty hours?"

"Anyone in mind, Miss Price?"

Her laugh was warm and full of promise. "Wait until you touch base, mister. Now, what can I do to help?"

Bolan gave her the location.

"I'll arrange for the local police to attend—welfare, too. Hal can liaise and make sure the women are taken care of. What are you going to do?"

"Wait around until I see the cavalry arriving. Then I'll slink off into the undergrowth and leave them to it. Talk to you later, Barbara," Bolan said and ended the call.

Back at the car, he explained the arrangements. The woman who spoke English listened, then translated for the others.

"We all thank you for what you have done," she said. Her dark eyes stared at him from the pale oval of her face. "Who are you? You do not look like a policeman."

"I'm a friend. Let's leave it at that. Where are you all from? The same place?"

"Yes. Chechnya. We were taken weeks ago and brought here to America. We are the last of the group. Others were moved on. We do not know where. Will you be able to help them?"

"I don't know. Maybe that man back there can be persuaded to talk," he said. "The police will try."

The woman nodded in resignation. "These are bad people. Very bad." Then she smiled and reached across the back of the seat to touch Bolan's hand. "I hope we can stay in America. There is very little for us back home. Thank you again."

Twenty minutes later, Bolan picked up the sound of approaching sirens and saw the multicolored flashing lights. He nodded to the woman.

"I have to go now. You'll be okay."

The woman watched him as he slipped from the car and eased into the shadows beyond the club. He was long gone when the cavalcade of police and welfare vehicles swept into the club parking lot.

7

Trenton, New Jersey

Harry Jigs drained his coffee mug and considered his next move. He knew what he wanted to do—dig out some more information he could pass along to Cooper. He felt he owed it to the man. Cooper had always been generous—more than generous—and despite his criminal tendencies, Harry Jigs considered himself an honorable man. Cooper wouldn't be expecting any additional information. He'd made a deal and paid up front. But Jigs figured there was no reason he couldn't throw in something extra.

He glanced at his watch. Just after midday. Across the street from the diner where Jigs sat, he could see the entrance to one of Marchinski's tawdry clubs. The street level was a low-rent strip joint. The second floor was where the main business was conducted. Up there was a fully equipped pornography studio. Jigs had sampled a number of their movies and even he found them hard to watch.

A little more information on this establishment would be just what Cooper was looking for. Jigs fingered the compact digital camera in his coat pocket. If he could get a few shots of people working in the movie setup, he'd be able to furnish Cooper with current intel.

Jigs had been watching the side alley ever since he'd entered the diner. In that time, no one had come or gone. Either the place was deserted, or they were all inside doing whatever it was they did. Jigs decided this was as good a time as any. He took out his cell phone and checked the battery then dropped the phone back in his pocket and left the diner, crossing the street.

Jigs quickly made his way down the alley. There were a couple of large, wheeled trash containers against the club wall and a little farther along, at the rear of the building, was a parking area with a few cars.

Jigs took out his phone and snapped a number of shots of the cars, making sure he got clear photos of the license plates. He took one of the building, as well. Jigs tapped out a text message, added the photos and sent the message to Cooper's cell phone. He dropped the cell back in his pocket. Crossing the parking area, Jigs made his way to the rear entrance.

There was a roller shutter door with a keypad fixed to the wall beside it. He studied it for a while, wishing he had the time to break the key code, but here and now—in broad daylight—was not the time to risk getting caught. A better chance would come later, when it got dark.

Jigs turned, ready to make his way back to the street, when he caught a shadowy glimpse of someone standing close by. He had barely registered the presence before something hard slammed across the back of his head. Jigs grunted as searing pain swelled up and he stumbled, falling against the wall of the club. The swiftness of the attack and the overwhelming pain left Jigs helpless.

"Come nosing around here, you sneaky little bastard, will you."

The words reached Jigs as if from a long way off. He tried to regain control of his weakened limbs. Something hit him again and Jigs slid to his knees. He felt hands take hold of him, pulling him upright.

"Want to see what's going on inside? We can do that for you, Jigs."

They knew his name.

A jolt of fear ran through Jigs.

His senses were off-line. Jigs had no idea who had hit him, nor did he understand what was going on. All he registered was the fact that he was being moved. Half dragged into a dimly lit passage. He drifted in and out of consciousness. The movement seemed to go on for some time. Then he felt himself being pushed off his feet. He slammed down on a hard surface and lay there in a daze.

Jigs heard distant sounds—muffled voices and the scrape of shoes on a hard surface. Someone stepped in close. The hard tip of a boot slammed into his side, driving the breath from Jigs's lungs. He cried out.

"Son of a bitch is still alive," someone said, laughing.

"Not for long—unless I find out what he's up to. I know this miserable piece of shit. His name's Harry Jigs, and he's been a pain in the ass for a long time. Wake him up—I need to have a talk with him."

"Hey, the boss doesn't want anything happening on the premises."

"So I'll take him somewhere quiet."

Jigs felt his wrists being pulled together behind his back and secured with a plastic tie. A larger loop was pulled tight around his ankles.

Hands took hold of him and he was lifted off the

floor, carried to a waiting car and pushed into the trunk. Jigs barely had time to register this before the trunk was slammed shut and he was in total darkness.

THE RIDE WAS ENDLESS. Jigs was jostled around inside the trunk. The air was hot, stale and tinged with the smell of gasoline. Sweat soaked him. The plastic ties around his wrists chafed and tore his skin. Jigs felt the slick warmth of blood run across his palms and seep between his fingers.

His body hurt. There was a pounding in his skull. Harry Jigs knew he was in trouble. He'd gone too far and now he was paying for his mistake. He had the feeling he might not survive whatever lay ahead.

Jigs knew Marchinski's reputation for violence. The mobster surrounded himself with hard people, and if anything was liable to enrage them, it was someone spying on their business. Cooper had cautioned him against doing anything foolish. Jigs should have heeded the man's advice. He had no one to blame except himself.

The pain in his head grew, and Jigs drifted into semiconsciousness. The car finally came to a stop, but for Jigs, the trunk being opened barely registered. He reacted when he was unceremoniously hauled out of the car and dropped onto another hard floor. Jigs was unable to hold back a groan.

His unseen captor leaned over him.

"Still with us, huh? That's handy 'cause I need to find out what the hell you've been doing."

Jigs felt himself being dragged across the floor. He was pulled to his feet and leaned against a pillar.

"Now don't you run away, Jigs."

His captor laughed at his own joke as Jigs felt something winding around his body—a rope securing him to the pillar and supporting him.

For the first time, Jigs was able to see his assailant clearly and when he recognized the man, Jigs was unable to hold back a shiver of fear.

Val Corbett was one of Marchinski's enforcers. Known for his unswerving loyalty and his vicious temperament, Corbett was a loner, preferring to carry out his duties on his own. He was said to enjoy his work almost too much, but Marchinski liked that quality.

"You know me, Harry," Corbett said with a smile. "Do yourself a favor and let's get this over with." That laugh again. "Not too fast, though. I haven't had much personal business lately."

Jigs sucked in a shivering breath as he stared at Corbett. A cold, hard fact hit him—he wasn't going to talk his way out of this. Val Corbett did not make deals. He did his job plain and simple.

Jigs watched the man pull on black leather gloves. Corbett was still smiling as he moved in close and began to hit Jigs. The enforcer knew how to inflict the maximum pain without causing any fatal damage. After all, he wanted Jigs to talk.

The beating lasted for a few minutes.

Corbett was sweating nicely when he stepped back.

Jigs was bleeding profusely. One eye was swollen shut and his nose had been broken. Bruises were starting to show on his cheeks and jaw. His mouth was awash with blood, and more bruises were forming over his ribs.

Corbett took hold of Jigs's hair and lifted his head.

"Harry, I need a break. You know how hard it is to keep this up?"

Jigs stared at him through his good eye. He hurt. He

felt sick. He could feel the blood running down his face and taste it in his mouth.

"I don't know what you want," he mumbled; he found it hard to speak because his lips were already badly swollen and split.

"I want you to tell me who you've been speaking to. Don't lie to me, Harry, you were seen. You were having a long conversation with this big guy in a diner—black hair, tough-looking dude. He gave you a nice thick envelope. And you wrote something down for him on a paper napkin. And now here you are scoping out one of Mr. Marchinski's spots."

Jigs shook his head.

"Harry, don't play games with me. We know you were with this guy. And you know what else? Things have been happening since you talked to your friend. Bad things, Harry. We got hit—real hard. It cost us men and money. You meet this guy, you talk, money is handed over, you give him something and suddenly our places get hit. Who is he, Harry? A cop? Fed? This isn't looking good for you."

Corbett let go of Jigs's hair and stepped back a little. Then the beating started again. This time the blows were harder. Blood cascaded down Jigs's front, soaking his shirt. He passed out.

Jigs was brought out of his semiconscious state by a sharp pain that seemed to engulf his body. He jerked in a spasm. The pain continued, and he was unable to hold back a scream.

Corbett had torn away his shirt and was cutting deep gashes in Jigs's lean, naked torso. The cuts were painful but not severe enough to kill. Blood was flowing from the wounds caused by the razor-sharp lock knife Corbett was wielding.

"You're back with me. That's good," Corbett said, relishing the moment. "It's time you started speaking, Harry, because I'll be running out of space to cut. Just give me a name and I'll stop. Tell me who you snitched to, then it can all be over."

Jigs stared at the enforcer. He knew in that moment he was going to die very soon. Corbett would not allow him to survive. And Harry Jigs, even in the terror of the moment, would not give him what he wanted. He owed that much to Cooper. The man had always treated him decently, and he'd promised to use the information Jigs had given him to strike out at the Marchinski and Tsvetanov organizations. That had been good enough for Jigs then, and it was even now.

"I can tell you…" Jigs whispered through swollen, torn lips.

Corbett's smile showed. He moved closer to hear what Jigs was going to say.

Jigs spat a heavy mouthful of blood into the man's face—enough to film Corbett's eyes. Corbett uttered a shocked grunt and stepped back, dragging his sleeve across his blood-spattered face.

"Bastard," Corbett screamed, his rage wiping away any restraint.

And in his fury, he lost it. Anger swept over him, a red rage brighter than the blood streaking Harry Jigs's face and body.

Corbett lunged at Jigs, the blade of the lock knife plunging into his captive's chest over and over in a fit of uncontrolled savagery that only ended when Jigs's body slumped against the rope around him.

8

Trenton, New Jersey

Bolan felt his cell vibrate. He slipped it from his pocket and saw that he'd received a text message with a few attachments. Harry Jigs had sent him the location of a Marchinski business venture that made pornographic movies. The attachments showed a number of parked vehicles and their license plates. There was also a photo of the building.

Bolan tried to call Jigs, but no one picked up. He let the cell ring on. Nothing.

Harry Jigs was not answering.

Bolan contacted Stony Man and asked for Kurtzman. He didn't waste time on formalities.

"I'm sending you a cell number. Can you tell me where that phone is located right now?"

"Give me the data, Striker."

Bolan transmitted the information.

"I'll call you back," Kurtzman said when he received the transfer.

Bolan exited his motel room and sat behind the Suburban's wheel, motor running.

He was plagued by the feeling something was not right. Jigs had sent a message. Now he wasn't responding.

What the hell was Harry doing?

Bolan had told him not to do anything risky, to stay safe.

The cell rang. It was Kurtzman.

"Got you a fix," Kurtzman said. "The cell is on and stationary. I'm downloading the location and I'll tap the coordinates into your sat nav."

Bolan watched the route emerge and settle on the screen. He swept the lever into drive and felt the big vehicle start to move.

IT TOOK BOLAN just over forty minutes to reach the sat nav's designated location—an industrial area containing warehouses and clusters of storage units. Many of the units looked unused, dark and just this side of derelict. The complex itself stood way back from any main route.

Bolan left his SUV on the perimeter and made his way along the wide alleyways between the buildings.

This spot was a long way from the city address Jigs had texted to Bolan. Jigs didn't drive, so how had he ended up here? Bolan gripped his Desert Eagle. This was not about to end pleasantly.

The Executioner sensed something off-kilter about this place—the stillness and the sense of foreboding that often preceded an ambush. The feeling was palpable, and it made Bolan step carefully, heading toward the closed doors of the large unit in front of him.

Bolan placed a hand against one of the doors and pushed. The door swung open and allowed daylight to penetrate the interior.

The expansive room was empty, the floor scattered with debris and dust.

Bolan stepped inside.

No, he realized, it wasn't quite empty.

A slumped human form, sagging against the rope holding him to one of the warehouse's support pillars, broke up the emptiness.

Bolan didn't need to move closer. He recognized Harry Jigs before he'd taken a half-dozen steps inside.

He saw the blood that soaked the figure and pooled on the floor. He saw the savage, cruel slashes in Jigs's flesh. Someone had killed Jigs in a cruel way. When Bolan reached Jigs, he saw the swollen features where the man had been brutally beaten.

Jigs had died because he was trying to help Bolan. He'd been slaughtered. There was no other way to describe what had happened.

Harry Jigs might not have been a model citizen. He may not have been an example of honesty and integrity. He had, though, been straight with Bolan.

Now Jigs was dead.

Murdered simply because of his association with Mack Bolan. Tortured for any possible information he might have carried. It was a needless death carried out by someone harboring psychotic tendencies.

"Sorry, Harry," Bolan said quietly. "It won't go unpunished."

Bolan methodically checked Jigs's pockets. He found Jigs's cell in one of the deep pockets of the dead man's blood-soaked pants. The killer had obviously overlooked the cell.

Or had he?

Bolan considered the question. Would the killer have neglected to search Jigs? Or did he locate the cell, check its call list and consider there might be a follow-up? Had the cell been left in the hopes that the message might be traced?

In death had Harry Jigs become a lure? Left where he'd died to draw in another victim for the killer?

Bolan turned and made his way across the unit to the exit. He held the Desert Eagle down at his side, slightly concealed by his leg as he stepped outside. The concrete apron between the warehouses maintained a silence that might have been unnerving to others. Bolan eased away from the building.

Watching.

Listening.

He heard the soft growl of a hyped-up motor. It had a deep, powerful sound. The growl turned into a solid throb as the motor was boosted, followed by the squeal of tires on a concrete surface. Bolan turned as he fixed the position of the car, just in time to see it burst into view from the alley between a pair of long sheds. The vehicle, a bright red 1969 Dodge Charger, slid a fraction as the wheelman brought it around to face Bolan. The rising howl of the motor emphasized the power under the hood. Smoke streamed in the Charger's wake as the driver pushed down on the accelerator and the car sprang forward, coming at the Executioner in a straight, controlled line.

In the brief splinter of time before he threw himself out of harm's way, Bolan recognized the car. It was one of the vehicles in the images Jigs had sent.

Bolan managed a shoulder roll, hitting the concrete smoothly, coming to rest and pushing to his feet. The Desert Eagle was still in his hand. Bolan turned about as he leveled the big semi-auto pistol, finger curling against the trigger as he focused on the rear end of the Dodge.

The pistol slammed out a pair of .44 caliber slugs that cored through the right rear tire. Chunks of rubber blew out as the tire ripped open. The Dodge dropped onto its alloy rim and the vehicle fishtailed. It lurched across the concrete, slamming against the side of one of the buildings. The front wheels twisted to the left, burying the nose of the car in the unit wall. The auto gave a shuddering jerk and came to a dead stop.

Bolan was already moving, making a hard run in the direction of the stalled car. He was only a few feet away when the driver's door was kicked open and an armed figure began to push himself clear. The man gripped a pistol in his gloved right hand, swinging it at Bolan as he spotted the tall figure approaching.

The distance closed within seconds.

The driver pushed himself upright.

Bolan reached out with the Desert Eagle and slammed the heavy weapon across the hardman's gun hand. Something cracked. The man gave a startled cry, the pistol dropping from his numb fingers. His left hand dipped into the pocket of his jacket and came out gripping a lock knife, his thumb opening the blade. As it locked into place, Bolan sidestepped, launching a powerful kick with his right foot. The driver felt the impact as Bolan's boot connected with his hand. The force of the blow angled the man's arm up, fingers losing their grip on the knife. It hit the car roof and slid out of sight.

"Sonofabitch." The word erupted from the man's lips as he took a wild swing at Bolan, ignoring the Executioner's weapon. Bolan leaned away from the badly judged blow, then slammed the big .44 down across the base of the man's exposed skull. The blow was hard, landing with a meaty thump, and the guy went facedown on the ground.

Bolan retrieved the dropped handgun and tucked it behind his belt. He took hold of the moaning man's collar and hauled the semiconscious figure upright, slamming him against the side of the car.

"You finished playing games?" Bolan asked.

"The hell with you."

Bolan rapped the guy across the cheek with the solid Desert Eagle. "Wrong response."

"Try go fuck yourself, then."

"I like it when you guys decide to play tough."

Bolan used his bunched left fist, cracking it against the man's mouth. He drew blood as the hardman slid sideways, his knees bending.

"Jesus, hell, that hurt," he yelled, scrabbling awkwardly as he attempted to stay on his feet.

"That was the intention."

The guy pawed at his bleeding mouth. That was when Bolan saw the dried blood on the leather of his gloves. It was heavy and recent. Bolan recalled the beating Harry Jigs had received.

Corbett stared at the tall dark-haired figure standing over him, deciding that getting his face turned inside out wasn't worth it. One look into those intense ice-blue eyes convinced him he'd lose more than he was prepared to risk.

"Harry Jigs," Bolan said. "What did he do that got him killed?"

Val Corbett couldn't hold back a crooked grin as he played a mental image of what had happened to Jigs.

"Poked his nose in where he didn't belong. Should have known better." Then Corbett regained a little of his brash attitude. "I made him realize his mistake…"

"Don't know when to quit, do you? Figure the protection Marchinski provides makes you invincible?" Bolan spoke quietly, his tone almost soothing.

"If you mess with Marchinski, you bring a heap of trouble down on yourself."

"You think?" Bolan said.

"Hell, I know. All you got to do is remember what happened to Jigs."

"I do remember," Bolan said, taking a step back.

It finally dawned on Corbett that he'd said too much, and he made a desperation play, lunging for Bolan. The .44 Magnum pistol cracked once, the slug slamming between the guy's eyes. It chewed its way through the skull and took a sizable chunk with it. The bloody spatter streaked the Dodge's roof as the guy dropped, jerking in final spasms. He flopped loosely at Bolan's feet.

Bolan leaned inside the car and picked up the cell he'd spotted on the passenger seat. He checked the call list and saw the dead man had made a connection only minutes before Bolan had reached the rendezvous. Bolan hit redial, and the call was answered quickly.

"You get it done already?"

"It's done," Bolan said. "Not the way you were expecting."

"You ain't Val."

"You picked up on that fast. Marchinski must be hiring smarter these days."

"Where's Val?"

"He won't be coming to the phone. Things got a little heated, and he kind of lost his head. Most of it's spread over his car."

"Bastard. You're making things hard for yourself, you…"

"Just tell your boss, Tsvetanov says it's time for him to quit. He should be getting the message by now."

Bolan ended the call. He dropped the cell on the ground and crushed it beneath his boot.

Then he walked away, easing into the shadows and back through the silent buildings to where he'd left his own car.

The area was isolated and Bolan didn't expect anyone to have heard the shots. He couldn't guarantee that, but he had the feeling Corbett's body would lie undetected for some time. At least long enough for Marchinski's people to discover the corpse.

He thought of Harry Jigs—a little guy simply trying to make his way on the fringes of the criminal world. He wasn't a violent man, more a trader of information. He had made a living out of it, too. But when he stepped into the Marchinski/Tsvetanov arena he'd inadvertently moved up the ladder—out of the shadows and into the light. Jigs's attempt to settle old scores had painted a target on his back.

Bolan felt regret.

He had brought Jigs into the spotlight by asking for information.

The Executioner always tried, and often succeeded, to keep innocents away from harm. Sometimes the opposite happened, and the Harry Jigses of the world became victims.

When that happened, Bolan grieved for them. He could not simply ignore those losses. They would be remembered and somewhere, sometime, Bolan would honor those dead in his own way. Right there and then, there was little else he could do.

"It's done, Harry," Bolan said, knowing that the simple words were far from enough to erase the debt.

9

Marchinski Residence

Gregor Marchinski took the news of Val's death far better than expected. The truth was he didn't really give a damn that the man was dead. Val Corbett had been an employee, nothing more, and getting himself killed showed he hadn't been up to the job. There were plenty more guns for hire. Besides, Gregor had important matters on his mind.

He needed to get his brother out of prison. Nothing else mattered. Dead employees, business, upcoming contracts, they all faded into the background.

Gregor wanted his brother back. Leo was the driving force behind the Marchinski organization. He had the strength to run things. The vision. The authority. It had always been that way. Even when they were children, Leo had been the one to lead and Gregor the one to follow.

More important, Leo looked out for his younger brother. He protected Gregor, kept him safe and even killed for him.

The brothers Marchinski had risen through the criminal ranks to form their own organization, quickly establishing themselves as untouchable. As they gained in notoriety, lesser groups, those who'd stood against them, were quickly dealt with. It became known to the criminal fraternity that Marchinski Incorporated was not to be taken lightly. Resistance would trigger a lethal response, and any group would find itself under the hammer if it dared to stand against the brothers.

With Leo in prison, Gregor was in charge—on the surface. It was not a position he wanted. There was too much responsibility. Too many decisions to make. It didn't help that Gregor failed, as always, in having the full backing of the rank and file.

Even though Leo was not present, his powerful influence over his people kept them from doing anything too drastic where Gregor was concerned. Leo's organizational skills meant the business ran smoothly, and Gregor was looked on as little more than a figurehead.

Gregor's real ally was Lazlo Sabaroff. The burly, physically powerful man had been Leo's rock, but with Leo out of the picture—and Gregor unable to fill his older brother's shoes—Sabaroff had stepped up. He'd helped the younger Marchinski to keep control of the organization.

Sabaroff had engineered the kidnapping of Mason's young daughter. Once Leo had come up with the plan, Sabaroff had the girl taken and the nanny killed. He'd delivered the telephone messages to Mason, making it clear what would happen if Leopold Marchinski was kept locked up.

Lazlo Sabaroff had been a true and loyal friend to Gregor Marchinski.

But, of course, outward appearances could be deceptive.

10

Maryland

Going for the head of the snake meant taking decisive action. There was no time for hesitation.

Working a lead provided by Harry Jigs, Bolan was moving in on a rural Maryland farmhouse that was part of the Marchinski empire.

Bolan circled the property and moved in with characteristic single-mindedness. He crossed the perimeter, silent and dark, his presence not noted by the first of the armed hardmen.

The gunman was tramping his path, probably for the dozenth time, and gazing straight ahead. His lack of concentration was his undoing.

Bolan rose out of the gloom, directly behind the unsuspecting sentry, who only became aware of the Executioner when Bolan looped an arm around his neck, drawing him in tight and bearing down against the back of his skull with his free hand. As Bolan applied pressure, he felt the man begin to struggle. It was a futile gesture. Already, Bolan's deadly grip was closing him down, shutting off his airway, and the man's frantic twisting and turning simply sped up the process.

Bolan leaned back, lifting the man's feet off the

ground so that his weight was concentrated on the mus-
cled arm around his neck, crushing the bones and shutting off the flow of blood. The sudden heavy weight of
the sentry told Bolan it was over. He eased the lifeless
form to the ground, quickly stripping away the sentry's weapons.

Bolan had his own ordnance, but extra firepower
could not be overlooked. Bolan tucked the pistol, a 9 mm
Glock, into his belt. He snatched up the dropped SMG,
checking the load for the Heckler & Koch MP5. The
acquired weapons added to his hip-holstered Desert
Eagle and the shoulder-holstered Beretta 93R.

Bolan slung his Uzi across his back, took hold of the
dead man's collar and dragged him out of sight behind a
clump of tangled vegetation. With the MP5 in his hands,
Bolan crouched and observed the layout.

The farmhouse was on his left. Farther on and yards
behind the baseline of the house was the barn, a sturdy,
Dutch-style construction with the timber painted ma-
roon and white. There was even a mid-sized stable and
beside it, an empty corral. The whole complex looked
to be in reasonable condition, but there was a deserted
air hanging over the place; this was no working estate.
The only signs anyone might be in residence were the
vehicles parked outside the house; Bolan counted three
high-end SUVs.

The Marchinski organization was supposedly using
the property as a halfway house. It might have been the
twenty-first century, but these human carrion never
changed. They operated on the fringes of the law—
taking, never giving—and used the age-old tricks of
the trade.

Even now they worked on human frailty, the hunger for drugs and illicit temptations. Be it liquor, porn,

women or stolen goods, the Marchinskis of the world were always ready to hand it out. At a price, of course. Unfortunately, there was always a ready market. People never tired of the forbidden—the quick buy or the lower price…ownership of something illegal. There was always a risk, but that added to the thrill of getting one over on the good guys. In hard times, when the dollar had less buying power, being able to obtain something cheaper was worth the risk.

Those who traded with the mob only encouraged them, but in hard times people turned to whatever outlet they could find. Marchinski and Tsvetanov simply filled a need. They offered a deal and the consumers took it.

The drug and alcohol abusers had no choice at all. Once hooked, they would take whatever was on offer, with total disregard as to where the product came from. They had no way out of the hell they had fallen into. Addicts would lie and cheat, steal and sell themselves to get what they needed. Lives were ruined and families torn apart.

The endless flow of the businesses demanded more. It was, as ever, ceaseless.

Mack Bolan understood the evil. He faced it on a regular basis, doing what he could to stamp it out. Any triumph, however small, was just that. A victory in his everlasting war. Bolan knew he would never eradicate the world's sickness, but a single, albeit small, achievement made the struggle worthwhile.

In this case, that would be the return of Abby Mason to her father. The child had been drawn into a savage world and held as a pawn in a cruel game she should have no part in.

The Marchinskis had gone way over the line by kidnapping the girl.

Bolan would see to it they paid the ultimate price.
There would be no quarter.
No mercy.
Only the striking hand of Mack Bolan.
The Executioner.

BOLAN HEARD THE CAR approach, the sound rising as it curved into view and headed toward the house. He eased back into the undergrowth and watched as the Ford sedan rolled to a stop alongside the SUVs. The driver's door swung open and a tall, lean man with a shock of corn-colored hair stepped out, unfolding his six-six frame. He turned back to the car and made a sharp gesture.

Three figures emerged from the rear. Two men escorted the third, who had his hands secured behind him. The captive moved slowly, obviously in some pain. His escorts had to take hold of his arms and haul him upright. They followed the tall man in the direction of the house and were met by a man in his shirtsleeves who emerged from the front door. There was a short exchange before the newcomers followed the guy from the house in the direction of the barn.

Bolan was assimilating this when he became aware of a new figure who'd appeared from the far side of the house. He was armed, carrying an MP5, and he stared in Bolan's direction, scanning back and forth. He was looking for the sentry Bolan had taken down.

The gunman started in Bolan's direction, the SMG brought into play as he closed in. He had a taut expression on his broad face, suggesting he was not happy with the situation.

The man stopped some ten feet from where Bolan

crouched. He looked left and right, even turned to check back the way he'd come.

"Rackham, where the hell are you? Show yourself."

The element of surprise was in danger of crumbling. Bolan had intended on getting in close and striking before the opposition could organize themselves. If this man raised the alarm, Bolan would have to battle every inch of the way.

The Executioner had a choice: let this man raise the alarm or stop him before he did.

The gunman moved two, three feet forward, bringing him even closer to where Bolan was concealed.

"That you, Rackham? What the—"

Bolan lunged forward, clearing the undergrowth in a powered surge. His tall figure erupted into view, and he was on the man before he could react fully.

Bolan slammed the body of his SMG into the man's face, the hard impact crushing his target's nose. Blood spurted and the man gasped against the sudden flare of pain. Bolan didn't allow him any opportunity to resist. He hit the gunman again, using the MP5 to inflict as much damage as he could, driving him back. Blood masked the man's features and his reactions were slowed.

Bolan's left boot drove forward, catching the man's knee. The blow was delivered with all of Bolan's considerable strength. The man gave a sharp squeal of pain as bone crunched and the limb collapsed. As he slumped forward, Bolan drove his right knee up into the already bloody face. The guy's head snapped back and he slammed to the ground, lying still.

Bolan stripped the man of his weapons, throwing them deep into the foliage. Then he turned toward the barn.

The bound captive interested Bolan. It was obvious

the man's trip to the barn was not for pleasure. He was in Marchinski's hands, and that was warning enough for Mack Bolan.

Keeping to the tree line, Bolan wound his way to the rear of the house, making sure there were no more sentries. He homed in on the distant structure.

Bolan came up to the side of the barn, and as he pressed against the timber, he picked up the subdued murmur of voices coming from inside the structure. There were also the unmistakable sounds of someone being struck—the meaty thwack of flesh being pounded.

Bolan checked the MP5, a final, automatic gesture that ensured the weapon was ready for use. He clicked the selector to 3-round burst.

A man screamed in pain.

It was a sound ripped from the very soul, and it galvanized Bolan into action. He made the final move from the side of the barn, crossing to the front and searching for access. The high doors were not fully closed, allowing Bolan to peer inside.

The generous interior was empty except for the men grouped around the captive. He had a rope looped around his chest, leading up to the thick cross-beam where he was suspended with his feet a few inches from the floor. His jacket and shirt had been stripped from his body, and his hands were still tied behind his back, leaving him powerless to avoid the leather-clad fists of one man who was systematically beating him around the face and body. Next to him, a man Bolan hadn't yet seen was wielding a slim-bladed knife. The blade was streaked with blood—showing it had been used—and the bloody wound in the victim's torso showed where.

Bolan slipped in through the gap in the doors, pressing tight against the wood to cover his back. The man wielding the knife moved forward, the gleaming blade catching light as he waved it back and forth.

"Put down the knife," Bolan ordered.

Every head turned at the sound of his words. All save the man with the blade. He ignored Bolan's command, and his arm moved as he prepared to strike again.

He'd been warned.

The MP5 moved, and its muzzle locked on to its target. Bolan stroked the trigger and put a three-round burst into the knife-wielding man's lower back. The trio of 9 mm slugs severed his spine, and he pitched forward onto his face, flopping around until his shattered body lost control and he lay still.

The others spread out, moving away from their prisoner. One man reached for the pistol worn at his waist, hauling the auto weapon clear as he began to turn in Bolan's direction. He caught Bolan's triple burst in the chest, the tight grouping ravaging his heart and dropping him to the barn floor.

The tall man, moving surprisingly fast for someone of his size, dropped to a crouch as he pulled a large auto pistol from under his coat and squeezed off shots in Bolan's direction.

But speed did not always mean accuracy. The heavy slugs ripped chunks out of the barn door inches from Bolan. He felt a flying piece of timber clip his cheek, drawing blood.

The Executioner stood his ground, tracking the gunman and hitting him with a triple-burst that opened the man's skull. The yellow hair was briefly streaked with bright blood before the head broke apart and spilled flesh, bone and brains. The man's eyes widened with the shock as he went down.

The group was down to two.

The man in his shirtsleeves flicked blood from his arm as he appraised the silent, menacing figure wielding the MP5. He had the look of someone used to giving orders and having them obeyed, and he faced Bolan without a tremor.

"I suggest we talk this over before anyone else gets hurt," he said.

"I suggest you cut that man down before you start giving orders."

He turned to his remaining crewman and gave a sharp nod. Bolan watched, unmoving, as the hurt man was lowered from the beam and his hands freed.

"Move over here," Bolan said and watched the freed captive cross the barn. When he was standing next to him, Bolan told him to pull the barn doors shut and secure them.

When he'd completed Bolan's request, the man leaned wearily against the closest door, one hand pressed to the knife gash in his torso.

"You should get him to a hospital before he bleeds to death," Shirtsleeves said.

"Suddenly, you're concerned," Bolan said. "Might restore my faith if I thought you meant it."

The man standing next to Shirtsleeves muttered something. His remark drew a harsh laugh from Shirtsleeves.

"Vince here wants me to distract you so he can shoot you," Shirtsleeves said. "I figure that would only get us both killed."

"Let him take his best shot," Bolan said. Then he added, "Vince, take out the gun and toss it." The MP5 covered the scowling man. "I don't ask twice."

Vince complied, throwing his auto pistol across the barn floor.

"Now the man's shirt and jacket."

The victim's clothing was rolled in a bundle and thrown across the barn. It landed a few feet from the injured man. He stepped slowly forward and retrieved the clothing. Bolan slid a hand into a pocket and drew out his lock knife. He passed it to the bleeding man.

"Cut some strips and tie a pad over the wound. Tie it tight, and it might slow the bleeding."

"All very touching," Shirtsleeves said, "but you should be worrying about the others in the house. If they heard the shooting they'll be wondering what's going on. There are a couple of outside guys, too…"

"You *had* guys outside," Bolan said.

"Tsvetanov is hiring smarter help these days."

Bolan made no effort to correct the man.

The injured man completed his makeshift bandaging and pulled his jacket back on.

"Best I can do."

"You able to hold a gun?" Bolan asked him.

The man nodded, and Bolan handed him the pistol he'd acquired.

Crossing the barn, Bolan used the discarded rope to secure the pair of Marchinski men. He led them to the far corner of the building, tied their feet and sat them down.

"Hey, this could be useful," Bolan's new ally said.

He offered his already cut shirt. Bolan took it and used his knife to sever the sleeves. He bound them around the two Marchinski men's mouths, gagging them firmly.

Then Bolan led the way to a small rear door, cracking it open and checking before he moved outside. They walked to the edge of the barn and looked at the house. There didn't appear to be movement, but Bolan didn't assume they were safe yet.

He turned to look at the man he had pulled out of trouble.

"What's your story?" Bolan asked. "What did you do to upset them?"

"Name's Tom Parker. ATF. I was working under-cover until I gave myself away. It was my own fault. A rookie mistake." He touched his bloody mouth, wincing at the pain. "I paid for that mistake. If you hadn't shown up, it would have been worse. I owe you…"

"Cooper."

"From? Karev figured you work for Tsvetanov. He got it right?"

"He was wrong."

"Then you're an Agency guy? FBI? Cop? I know you're not ATF."

"Let's just say if this were an old Western, I'd be wearing a white hat."

Parker managed a swollen smile. "Lone Ranger type, huh?"

"But don't expect the cavalry to charge to the rescue. I don't have backup on this."

"Hell, when you work undercover there never is a last-minute rescue."

Bolan agreed with that heartfelt sentiment. Over the years, on countless lone-wolf missions, Bolan had never expected help to arrive at the crucial moment. He oper-ated on a keen knife edge, orchestrating his incursions with a single-minded purpose and never anticipating the bugle call to say help was on its way. It was one man against the enemy, and there were times when those odds went over the top.

In the end, Bolan had only himself to depend on. He chose that path and would never regret taking it. He lived or died by his own game plan. Times were he came out by the narrowest of margins, often bruised and battered, but each time he walked away, he knew he had stepped ever closer to the edge.

"I take it you're not a fan of Marchinski and his business."

"His organization is in my sights. So is Tsvetanov's."

"Past time they were all taken down."

"So why don't we test the water, Agent Parker," Bolan said.

They cleared the barn and headed in the direction of the house.

A hunched figure came into view on the far side. The distance didn't prevent Bolan from recognizing the sentry he had put down using the MP5 like a club. The man's face was bloody, the lower half pushed out of shape. His damaged knee slowed him to a pained shuffle, but he broke into a run when he spotted Bolan and Parker. Closer to the front entrance he gave a yell, going up the steps to the shallow porch.

"No surprise, after all," the ATF agent said.

The front door swung open and a pair of armed figures appeared. The sentry waved frantically in Bolan and Parker's direction.

"Definitely no surprise," Parker said and brought his pistol into position.

Gunfire blanketed any more words.

The pair of Marchinski soldiers cut loose, the SMGs in their hands crackling harshly. The expended slugs chewed at the dusty yard, kicking up geysers of stones and dirt, falling only inches away from Bolan and Parker.

Bolan stood his ground, raised the MP5, acquired his target and stroked the trigger. He felt the vibration as the SMG fired. His three-round burst caught his target in the chest, knocking him backward. He struck the front of the porch wall, hanging motionless until his own body weight pulled him down.

In the seconds it took for Bolan to fire, Parker had double-fisted the Glock, picking his moment before he released three close shots—so close they sounded like one. The man on the receiving end tumbled down the porch steps and curled up.

The sentry broke into movement and snatched up the SMG that had been dropped on the porch. He was swinging it around for target location as he pushed upright.

Bolan put a three-round burst into his left side, the slugs splintering ribs as they chewed into his body. He slammed against the house, dropping to his knees, and the SMG slipped from his limp fingers.

"Hell of a neighborhood," Parker said. "There I was believing the countryside was clean and healthy."

He followed Bolan across the yard, where they cleared all the dropped weapons from the downed men.

Without a word, they flanked the open front door. The hallway inside was in half shadow. No sound. No movement.

"No more rats to drive out?" Bolan said. "Let's make certain."

They stepped inside, checking the house using a series of search-and-clear moves. Each downstairs room was breached and cleared, then the upper floor.

No people.

No Abby Mason.

But there was enough illegal material to keep the

ATF in business for a good while. Agent Parker looked over the stacked drugs, a half-dozen cases of MP5 SMGs and sealed cartons of ammunition.

"I might not have come across these the way I wanted," Parker said, "but I'm not complaining."

"Call it in, Parker. Get your people here before the Marchinski boys show up."

Parker spotted a few cell phones on a table, including his own. He picked it up and tapped in a number. As his call was answered, he wandered out of the house and stood on the porch.

Bolan picked up a second phone and entered the number that would connect him to Stony Man. When Price came on, Bolan asked to be transferred to Kurtzman. He told the cyber chief to download the cell's contents.

"What are we looking for, Striker?"

"Anything I can use," Bolan said. "I need a lead. Call me back on my own cell."

"You got it," Kurtzman said.

"When you're done, wipe the contents on this one. Everything."

Bolan didn't want anything left on the cell that might be picked up by the ATF.

There was a silence while Kurtzman locked his powerful equipment online, pulling the data on the cell Bolan was holding.

"I have it all. Now put the cell down because it goes dead any second."

Bolan glanced at the screen and saw it was clear. He switched off the cell and dropped it back on the table, knowing it was as clean as the day it had been purchased.

Parker entered the room, holding up his phone.

"This place will be swarming with an ATF crew in thirty minutes, Cooper. I get the vibe you'd rather not be here when they arrive. Would I be right?"

"What I'm looking for isn't here."

"Maybe I could help if I knew what it was."

The two men locked eyes for a moment and then Parker shrugged, realizing he would get nothing from Bolan.

"The old need-to-know clause?"

"Something like that. All I can say is an innocent life is at stake. I can't afford the holdups I'd get from your people. Too many questions I don't have the time to answer."

11

Washington, D.C.

It was the same metallic voice. Just listening to it sent a cold chill down Larry Mason's spine. He knew this was the man who had his daughter. The threat of death was hanging over his child. Even though he had been prepared for the call, it still tore through him.

"What do you have to tell me, Mason?"

Mason steeled himself and said, "Show me Abby first. Prove she's still alive and unharmed. If you don't, I take my chances and end this call."

The man laughed. "Still playing tough."

There was a pause, then a hesitant flicker and Mason saw Abby. She was sitting on a chair, holding up a copy of a newspaper. The image grew larger and Mason was able to read the date on the edition. The image drew back and now he could read the headline. It showed a current event.

Mason hoped the trace Brognola had set up was working correctly, and he was getting the same image and sound.

"Can she hear me?" he asked.

"No," the voice said. "But she can hear me. Nod for your father, Abby."

The child slowly nodded her head as she lowered the paper, staring fixedly into the camera. The expression on her pale face made Mason want to cry out.

The image vanished.

"Now we have established Abby is alive and unharmed, tell me what you have achieved so far. And remember, I have ears and eyes watching you. Do not play games with me, Mason."

"I'm trying to arrange for Marchinski to be moved from his current location to another facility. If I can do that, you'll have the chance to intercept him during the transportation and free him."

"That could be risky for us."

"There's risk for all of us. I risk losing my daughter. I risk being exposed and arrested for what I'm doing. You think this is a damned walk in the park for me?"

"Getting hostile is not gaining you any favors."

"Well, the hell with that," Mason said. "You put me in this position. Do you think I'm obliged to like it? I'll do what I can to carry out my side of this bargain. I have to believe you'll let Abby go if Leo Marchinski is freed. That's all I have to go on."

"Keep thinking that way, Mason."

"When I have more details, I'll give them to you. I can't push too hard or someone might start questioning my reasons."

"Just do it. And remember, the clock is ticking."

"When you call again, I'll be expecting an update on my daughter's condition. No Abby, no deal."

The voice held back for a moment. Then, "You keep pushing, Mason. Don't push too far."

"We already covered that. You need my input on this as much as I need my daughter alive. Just remember that."

The call ended.

Mason felt sweat running down his face. It slid under his collar, cold and clammy. He stared at the cell phone in his hand, fingers threatening to crush the thing. Mason took long breaths to steady himself.

When he felt calmer, Mason picked up the cell Cooper had given him and scrolled to the number for Brognola. His call was answered after the second ring.

"We got it all," Brognola said.

"What happens now?"

"I get the call analyzed. See if we can track the source of the signal. Have the voice run through specialist equipment. Try to break it down."

"Doesn't sound like you'll get instant results."

"I won't lie, Larry. These things take time. But the people on it are the best. If there's an answer, they will find it."

"Have you heard from Cooper?"

"He'll call in when there's something to tell." Brognola cleared his throat. "I understand you must be feeling pretty isolated right now. Probably wondering what the hell is going on. Larry, we're not sitting on this. I promise."

"I know. Don't think I'm not grateful, Hal. It's not being able to do anything…"

"I can't tell you anything to make it easier right now. Mind a suggestion?"

"Go ahead."

"Do whatever you can to give the impression you have the Marchinski break in the pipeline. These people say they have ears in your organization, so give them something that can be passed on. If they imagine you're working on Marchinski's release, it should give you more time."

12

Marchinski Residence

"Well?" Sabaroff said. The single word held enough of a threat to make the three men cower inwardly.

Lazlo Sabaroff's physical presence was often enough to subdue most men. At six feet tall, he was broad, with a deep chest and wide shoulders. His shaved head completed the picture of a man possessed of brute strength coupled with an intimidating presence. He was an ideal second in command, able to carry out Leo Marchinski's orders to the letter.

There was no doubting Sabaroff's intelligence, either. He was a sharp observer, yet he gave the impression of not listening too closely. Because of that, people tended to talk loosely around Sabaroff while he soaked up conversations, never forgetting the important points.

Leopold Marchinski trusted his lieutenant without question. Over the years, they had weathered setbacks, gang rivalry and the successes that followed. No one had been more shocked at Leo Marchinski's arrest and incarceration, but Sabaroff had stepped into the breach, ostensibly helping Gregor, but in fact taking control of the organization. His ascension was not contested—for two reasons. Sabaroff was the natural choice to stand in during Marchinski's absence. Secondly, no one had the nerve to openly challenge the man. They had all seen the effects of his anger. The unfortunate ones who stood in his way never forgot the treatment they received.

Sabaroff waited for someone to speak. He was standing in front of Leo Marchinski's desk. Gregor slumped in his brother's swivel chair. His slight frame was dwarfed by the large piece of furniture.

"Have you all been struck dumb?" Sabaroff asked.

"No," one of the three said lamely. "It's…"

"We expected this might happen," Sabaroff said. "With Leo in a cell, Tsvetanov has chosen his moment. We don't let him get away with it. We hit back. I don't care which of his places you take down. Just organize and do it. Make sure he knows we mean business."

Sabaroff turned to Gregor. He realized the three men were still there.

"You're waiting for a drum roll?"

"No."

"Then get the hell out of here and do the job you're paid for."

As the office door closed, Sabaroff swung around to face Gregor.

"Am I going to have trouble with you, as well?" he asked.

Gregor shook his head. His tanned face looked haggard, with darkening shadows beneath his eyes.

"When will we get Leo out?"

The question was asked often.

The answer was always the same.

"The situation is being handled. Gregor, I told you from the beginning this would be difficult. Mason is working on a solution, but we can't expect this to come together instantly. Much as I don't like it, we're going to have to be patient."

"Jesus, Lazlo, it's getting worse. My brother is in jail. We have Tsvetanov taking shots at us. All we need now is for the cops to knock on the door. We've had that undercover ATF son of a bitch work his way inside. What comes next?"

"The ATF agent has been dealt with. He's at the farm. We can make him talk and then the boys can feed him through the wood chipper. Just the way we've done before."

Gregor subsided a little.

"Maybe I can take a run up there. See how things are being handled."

Sabaroff smiled, nodding. Inside, he was curled up. Gregor was showing his true self.

As far as Sabaroff was concerned, Gregor was a sick little creep. He would enjoy watching the ATF man being disposed of. There was an unhealthy aura around Leo Marchinski's brother. He would never get his own hands dirty, but he got some kind of kick watching others being hurt. There were times Sabaroff wondered if Leo and Gregor were really brothers.

His thoughts were disturbed when someone knocked on the door.

"Yeah?"

The door opened and one of the crew stepped into the office. The expression on his face warned Sabaroff that the man was not bringing good news.

"What now? Did you come to tell me we're being done for tax evasion?"

"Relief crew just called from near the farm," the man said. "The place is swarming with ATF men and cops."

Sabaroff maintained his blank expression. This

wasn't the kind of news he wanted to hear. His only comfort was the knowledge that any of the men taken by the cops would keep their mouths shut and wait for the organization's lawyer. Jason Keppler was good at his job. He cost a lot of money, but the guy knew the law every which way from sundown.

"Get Keppler on the phone," Sabaroff said. "I need to talk to him. Now."

The bearer of bad news hesitated. The look on his face suggested he hadn't finished his delivery.

"What?" Sabaroff barked.

"That call we got over Corbett's cell. We checked it out. Corbett's dead. Somebody splattered his brains across the roof of his Charger. And Harry Jigs's body was inside the warehouse where Corbett had him."

There was a half groan, half nervous laugh from Gregor. Sabaroff dismissed the messenger, then glanced at the younger Marchinski.

"Don't you get the feeling this isn't our day?" Gregor said. "Maybe even our damned year."

"These things happen," Sabaroff said. He couldn't think of any other response.

Sabaroff wouldn't allow it to show, but he admitted to himself that the situation was heating up. Too many things were going wrong. Isolated, they might not have been all that serious, but adding them together made Sabaroff more than a little nervous.

Maybe it was time he worked on righting the balance—letting Tsvetanov and his crew know they couldn't keep hitting the Marchinskis and get away with it.

Lazlo Sabaroff had his own personal agenda to work on. But until the right moment, he needed to keep things running as normally as possible. For now, he needed to send a message by taking a piece of Ts-vetanov's business and destroying it.

Baltimore Docks, Maryland

A COUPLE OF hours later, a black panel truck swept in from the road and headed for the dock area. The rain had been drifting in most of the afternoon. Now a down-pour was coming in off the water in sheets, falling from a cloud-ridden, darkening sky. Raindrops bounced off the dock and hammered at the buildings edging the area.

This was Tsvetanov territory. Merchandise came in by sea, was unloaded at the dock and either stored in the buildings or put into waiting vehicles for swift distribution.

A security detail oversaw the dock facility. The men were supplied with uniforms and equipment by the Tsvetanov organization, and the vehicles that patrolled the area also belonged to Drago Tsvetanov. The whole unit was managed by a company set up by Tsvetanov—trading under a different name.

The panel van parked well away from the patrolled area, the Marchinski crew moving in under cover of rain and the encroaching darkness.

There were six men—all dressed in black, with ski masks pulled over their faces. They were all armed with suppressed 9 mm Uzi SMGs and similarly suppressed 9 mm Beretta pistols. One man carried a backpack that held prepared blocks of C4 explosive compound.

Early intelligence had furnished them with the exact numbers of the Tsvetanov detail. There were three security guards on patrol around the facility. Inside the building, there was a work crew consisting of five men, with a further three armed guards overseeing the operation.

Late in the afternoon, a motor launch had delivered a consignment of Colombian cocaine. As soon as it had been transferred to the warehouse, the cutting crew began their work. The bulk cocaine would be weighed, cut and poured into smaller plastic bags for distribution to the dealers covering the city.

The Marchinski crew shot the outside security guards with silent, gas-powered pistols loaded with cyanide darts. The three men were dead seconds after they fell to the ground outside the guard station. Once the crew breached the fence, the bodies were quickly moved out of sight behind the parked security cars.

The man leading the crew had once been a member of the Russian military. Four years ago, when his army unit had been disbanded, Vertikov had found himself without a place in society…until he'd been approached by one of Marchinski's people. Within a month, Vertikov had been brought to America and provided with papers, a place to live and money in his pocket. Vertikov started working for his new employer immediately and soon proved his worth. He enjoyed his new position. It allowed him to resurrect his old skills, and today he was about to use those skills.

Vertikov dispersed his team. They moved fast, silently covering the warehouse frontage. Using hand signals, Vertikov assigned two of his men to guard the exterior before leading the others in through the access door.

The four armed men were able to enter easily, sticking to the shadows at the edges of the cavernous interior. Most of the space inside was taken up by stacks of crates and barrels, which were used to convey the impression this was simply a transit warehouse. The current activity was taking place farther into the building, where overhead lights cast yellow illumination over the drug operation.

Three guards were moving around the long tables, which held the drugs, while the five-man transfer crew doctored the powder, dividing the cocaine into smaller bags and packing those into boxes. Each of the workers wore filter masks to prevent the drugs from being inhaled. They also wore thin rubber gloves.

Vertikov led his men close to the working area, though they remained in the shadows. His hand signals indicated he wanted them to target the three armed guards. When he was satisfied his people were fully in position, Vertikov gave the signal.

The suppressed Uzis crackled and sent volleys of 9 mm slugs. Caught unprepared, the three guards were dropped without any chance of retaliating. They crumpled to the warehouse floor, bodies punctured by the 9 mm bursts.

The moment the guards had been dealt with, Vertikov's men stepped out from cover and surrounded the stunned workers.

From behind his ski mask, Vertikov spoke for the first time since arriving.

"Do it," he said.

The crew raised their Uzis and the dull rattle of suppressed auto fire echoed around the warehouse. The five workers were taken down, blood staining their clothing as the slugs tore into them.

"The explosives," Vertikov snapped, and the man with the backpack nodded.

He shrugged off the bag, opened it and took out the prepared explosive packs. There were four of them. He placed one on the main table where the drug consignment sat and spread the others around the warehouse. Once that was done, Vertikov ordered his crew out.

The men exited the warehouse, climbed back into the van, stripped off their masks and dropped them and their weapons into a large carry bag. There was no hurry, no panic. The explosive packs were set to detonate in fifteen minutes. That gave the crew ample time to get clear without having to rush. The last thing they wanted was to be seen driving away recklessly.

THE COMBINED EFFECT of the explosive packs demolished the warehouse. The resultant blaze spread across the dock and ignited other buildings. It took the efforts of three fire units to tackle the inferno.

It was not until the following morning, when the rain finally stopped, that the fire department was able to check out the gutted buildings. It took them most of the morning to work their way through the smoking debris to the bodies inside. The firefighters had already discovered the dead security men who'd been left behind the parked vehicles. Even they had been partly burned by the heavy blaze.

The fire marshal and his team slowly began to piece together what had happened, and their investigation moved up a notch once they realized the bodies inside the warehouse had been shot....

Stony Man Farm

HAL BROGNOLA READ through the report passed to him by Aaron Kurtzman. The Stony Man cyber team had picked up the story from news reportage and followed through by intercepting FBI and police details. With

his unerring capacity to locate and filter data, Kurtzman had compiled a concise package for Brognola. As
a legitimate civil servant high up in the Justice Department, Brognola had his own sources and by the late
afternoon—the day after the incident—he had a com-
prehensive rundown.

At first, Brognola thought he was looking at a Bolan
strike. The first reports had identified at least two of the
bodies as members of the Tsvetanov crime mob. On-
the-spot fingerprint checking, using a handheld Bio-
metric Fingerprint Reader, found a number of prints
that were identified via AFIS with two names—they
were known members of the Tsvetanov criminal organization. Brognola knew the Marchinski and Tsvetanov mobs were on Bolan's list, but he chose to speak
with his friend first.

"Is this anything to do with you, Striker?" he asked
once he had Bolan on the secure line and had detailed
what had taken place.

"Not guilty," Bolan said, and for Brognola, that was
enough.

"Then it's looking as if your strategy is working."

"So it does. I expect you're reading official reports."

"Interesting stuff. There's more to come," Brognola
said, "but fire department and FBI analysis at the scene
has already identified the presence of cocaine and C4
explosive."

"I'll hazard a guess this was a Marchinski strike
against Drago Tsvetanov."

"I'd have to say your disruptive influence has something to do with this, too."

"Getting them rattled was always part of the plan."

"Gregor Marchinski and his buddy Sabaroff will

have their hands full. Do you think it will take the heat off Mason and Abby a little?"

"Getting big brother out of jail will still be on the agenda," Bolan said, "but what's happening on the streets is going to distract them. Hopefully, it might just give me a little more stretch."

"Keep in touch, Striker. Anything breaks at this end, I'll let you know."

13

When Bolan had finished speaking to Brognola, he was transferred to Aaron Kurtzman. Bolan had his cell in the cradle on the dash, set on speaker. His eyes were fixed on the road ahead as he listened to Kurtzman's report. ·

"The guy sending Mason those messages has been identified as Lazlo Sabaroff—Leo Marchinski's lieutenant. After the voice analyzer broke down the sample, it searched for a match. Sabaroff was identified from a sound bite he did on the court steps after Marchinski was arraigned."

"So we have our source," Bolan said. "Anything on the phone signal?"

"Not so easy. Akira is working flat out trying to pin it down," Kurtzman said, referring to Akira Tokaido, an extremely gifted hacker who was a key member of the Farm's cyberteam. "The call came in via a spider web of signals. It was rerouted through providers worldwide. Marchinski must have a top-line tech man on his payroll." Kurtzman let the words sink in. "No way we can fast track this, Striker, but we won't give up. Boy Wonder will crack it."

"Anything else?"

"We're scanning the phone image showing the Mason

girl. There's nothing definite so far—just a plain room.
I'd say a bedroom."

"What about the newspaper?"

"I knew you'd ask. It's not a national. I'd say it's a
local rag. We're trying to pin it down. Trouble is there's
nothing to say where it comes from. Just the name—
Daily News. They're not making it easy for us. I'm running a list of newspapers with that masthead. There
looks to be a long list. Leave it with me, Striker. I need
a mug of coffee to stimulate my brain cells. There are
a few ideas rolling round in there."

Bolan sighed. He understood the complexities Kurtzman and his team battled. The needle and haystack
came to mind. Even electronic searching had its bad
days. He curbed his impatience, pushed thoughts of
Larry Mason's child to the back of his mind. As much
as he wanted to snatch her back from the Marchinskis,
Bolan had to remain impartial.

"Thanks, Bear."

"So what next?"

"I don't intend to let our bad boys off the hook. I need
to stir them up some more, keep them wondering what's
going on—especially the Marchinski mob. I get them
nervous enough, they might start making mistakes."

"I have to ask, Striker. Couldn't you be making
things harder for the girl?"

"She's already at risk. I'm making a considered
choice here, kicking over a few rocks and seeing where
it takes me. It's either that or I stand back and let Mason's time run out without doing a damn thing. Either
way, Abby is under threat until I find her."

"I'm glad I don't have to make that choice. We'll pull
out all the stops—push until something cracks wide-
open."

"Hell, I know that. You guys always work that way so what's different this time?"

Kurtzman offered a deep chuckle. "Now you're just trying to flatter me so I'll do my damndest."

"Is it working?"

"His fingers are a blur on the keyboard," Barbara Price said over the conference line. "Any minute now, I'll see steam rising."

"Yeah, okay," Bolan said. "I'm suitably humbled."

14

New York

"I don't know whether this will be of help," Kurtzman said. "It came up while we were trawling through that cell you wanted checking out. There was a hell of a lot of junk we had to filter through, but after we deleted the garbage, we were left with a few texts in some Russian subdialect. I had the texts translated and I'm sending the one you'll be interested in, Striker."

"I'll take a look."

The message came through on Bolan's cell minutes later. It detailed a meeting between two people, and one of the names was vaguely familiar. It brought Bolan back to Harry Jigs's scribbled data. Vorchek. Danton Vorchek. Jigs had him down as a drug dealer for the Marchinski mob. He was low on the ladder, working where he lived—the poorer sections of the city. Despite working a low-income spot, Vorchek pulled in substantial sums of cash. He ran a busy crew of dealers.

Kurtzman had run a make on Vorchek and had come up with the man's police file and—more important for Bolan—an address. Vorchek lived in one of the tenements in the underdeveloped section of the city.

Midmorning, Bolan left his Suburban streets away

and walked to the area. He'd dressed down for the visit—dark pants and a faded gray shirt under a loose jacket. His only nod to his normal dress code was the 93R in its shoulder rig beneath the thick jacket. Bolan wasn't going in loaded for bear, but he wasn't going to step into unknown territory unarmed.

Hands in his jacket pockets, Bolan mingled with the locals. He kept his head down, never meeting anyone's eye, and despite a few mumbled challenges, he met no hostility.

The apartment building was shabby and in need of a makeover. Bolan went up the worn stone steps and in through the front door. It took him into a dimly lit hallway, with uncarpeted stairs leading to the upper floors. The air was close and had a stale smell to it. Bolan made his way up to the third floor and followed the passage to Vorchek's door.

At some time in the past, there might have been a coat of paint on the cracked wood. Now the only decoration was a badly drawn number indicating it was the correct apartment.

Bolan paused, leaning in close. He couldn't hear any sound from inside the apartment. The brief rap sheet Kurtzman had downloaded told Bolan that Vorchek was a user as well as a dealer. If he was home, he might not even be fit to answer the door.

Bolan slipped his right hand under his jacket and gripped the butt of the Beretta. He decided to try the handle before knocking. The door gave freely. Bolan eased it open, surprised there was no creak from the dry hinges. He slipped inside and quietly closed the door behind him. There was a key in the lock, so Bolan turned it—it was safer than leaving the door open for anyone to come in behind him.

The apartment was sparsely furnished, and from a quick look, Bolan figured everything had come from junk stores; nothing matched and the furniture had the appearance of being well beyond new.

Bolan pulled the Beretta. He swept the room, stepping softly to minimize the creaking from the floorboards, then checked out the doors he could see. Two on his left. A single one on his right.

As Bolan looked around the room, he caught a fragment of movement from the partly open door on his right.

Someone was behind the door.

"That you, Vorchek? Get out here. I need to talk to you."

The door moved a fraction. The fleeting figure stepped away from the frame.

"I know you're in there. Better you come out. If you don't, it isn't going to be healthy for you."

Bolan's words had the desired effect. The door opened and the guy who came into view made Bolan imagine he was looking at his old informant Harry Jigs.

Danton Vorchek must have been in his late forties, though his drug habit made him look older. His skin was pale and blotchy, and graying hair barely covered his scalp. He stared at Bolan through watery eyes sunk in wrinkles. The shirt and pants he wore didn't look as if they'd been removed for months.

Vorchek came into the room, staring at Bolan with unconcealed suspicion.

"Never seen you before," he said. His Russian accent was pronounced.

"We've got that in common, then," Bolan said.

Vorchek scratched at the loose flesh under his unshaven chin. He gazed around the room as if it was unknown to him.

"Have you come to steal from me? If you have, it is a wasted journey."

"I'm here for information."

Vorchek's head dipped in a slightly mocking motion. He gave a dry chuckle.

"Do I look like an information bureau? You should go and buy a book." He paused. "What kind of information?"

Without waiting for Bolan to answer, Vorchek shuffled across the room. He stopped at a battered table and picked up a bottle of vodka, holding it up for Bolan to see.

"This is real vodka," he said. "All the way from Moskva. You want?"

"No."

"You should be more friendly. If you want information you should be…" Vorchek's head snapped around and he suddenly became very aware. "Are you cop? *Politsiya?*"

His left hand slid into his pocket, pulling out a switchblade knife. Bolan saw the slim, gleaming blade snap into position. Vorchek placed the bottle back on the table. He rounded on Bolan, the knife held in a threatening position as he moved across the room.

"I think you are a damn cop. Maybe I carve a badge for you on your face."

The previously slow figure moved with deceptive ease. Even the weary eyes took on a brighter gleam. Vorchek's act vanished, and Bolan was faced with a real threat.

He let the Russian get close, watching the weaving blade. Vorchek came within a couple of feet before

Bolan moved. His right hand emerged from his jacket, the Beretta 93R flashing in a powerful arc. The weapon chopped down across Vorchek's arm above the wrist, delivered with all of Bolan's strength. Vorchek gave a scream as the heavy metal crunched against his flesh. Bone cracked. The knife slipped from Vorchek's grasp. Bolan kicked it across the room. He caught hold of Vorchek's shirtfront and swung the man aside, hurling the Russian into the table. He sprawled across it, and the rickety legs gave way. Vorchek went to the floor, the uncorked bottle of liquor falling with him. The clear liquid began to pour from the neck of the bottle, spreading across the bare floorboards.

Bolan reached down and caught hold of Vorchek's shirt collar. He dragged the moaning figure upright and deposited him in one of the mismatched armchairs. Vorchek hugged his fractured arm to his chest, gripping it with his free hand. A torrent of unchecked Russian poured from his lips and none of it came from Chekov's written works.

Bolan picked up the switchblade and let Vorchek see it. Sweat beaded the man's sallow face.

"Very handy piece of steel," Bolan said. He holstered the Beretta. "Could save me some ammunition."

"You cannot do that," Vorchek said. "American cops are not allowed to do such things."

"See, I thought you were a peaceful kind of guy," Bolan said. "I was wrong. Now you're making the same mistake. Who said I was a cop?"

"You said…"

"I said I wanted to ask questions is all."

"What questions?"

"Where's the drug house?"

Vorchek's expression changed. It was obvious that was not the question he'd been expecting, and it threw him.

"You want to steal drugs? From Marchinski?" Vorchek smiled, showing his misshapen, stained teeth.

"Where is the drug house?"

"You must be stupid. Crazy. No one takes from Marchinski. You try and you will die, idiot."

"I don't want to steal," Bolan said.

He leaned in close, the tip of the blade stroking Vorchek's cheek, scraping the sweating flesh and leaving a faint, bloody line.

"Then what? You want to buy?"

"No. I want to destroy it. Wipe it out. Burn it if I have to."

This time Vorchek's laughter was long, loud and unchecked. He seemed to have forgotten his fractured wrist, finding Bolan's statement highly amusing.

Bolan said nothing, simply allowing the man to finish.

When Vorchek returned to the Executioner's fixed stare, he sobered as he realized Bolan was serious.

"This is madness. You think you can walk in and destroy a Marchinski organization?"

"It's already happening."

"You? You are the one who has been hitting Marchinski?"

"Let's say I've been moving his organization along the road to redemption."

"I cannot believe this. You expect me to give up my friends?"

"Tell me or die. Simple as that. Ending your life means nothing to me."

"You will not kill me. You Americans are too soft."

Bolan stared at the switchblade. He didn't want to

do it, but he needed answers fast. The soldier closed the knife and dropped it into a side pocket, then reached under his jacket for the 93R, pointed it at Vorchek and pulled the trigger. The 9 mm Parabellum round sliced through the fleshy part of Vorchek's right thigh in a neat through and through. The suppressed auto pistol made little more than a hard thwack.

The Russian drug dealer clutched his free hand to the wound, gasping in shock. His fingers were instantly soaked in bright blood.

"You bastard," Vorchek squealed, his voice high and trembling.

Bolan moved the Beretta's muzzle and targeted Vorchek's other leg.

"Then your arms," he deadpanned. "Then…"

Vorchek watched the patch of blood on his pants spreading, thickening.

"I'll bleed to death if I do not get to a hospital."

"Then you know what to do."

"Send for an ambulance, then I'll tell you."

Bolan shook his head. "Talk first and make it the truth. Screw me, and I'll be back for you."

Bolan angled the Beretta, targeting Vorchek's knee. He kept his finger on the trigger.

"Hell of an impact from one of these," he said. "It'll make mush out of your knee. You'll be lucky if you ever walk on that leg again—muscle torn out, nerves shredded, bone in little fragments."

"Enough," Vorchek said, face ashen, skin wet with sweat. "You win. You win."

He gave Bolan the location. Vorchek was close to passing out from blood loss by the end.

"Now you call for an ambulance."

Bolan stepped back, eyes fixed on the dealer. There

was a cold finality in his expression as he moved the 93R and lined it up on Vorchek's head.

"You said you would send for help. For an ambulance."

"No. I never actually said that. But I'm going to make sure you're out of the picture." The soldier rapped the butt of the Beretta against the Russian's temple. He'd bind the man's entry and exit wounds, tie him up and call Brognola, requesting that the big Fed have the local P.D. pick up Vorchek. The last thing he needed was to have the guy make a call.

THE DRUG HOUSE was no better than Vorchek's apartment—a crumbling building that most wouldn't give a second look. The late afternoon lent it an even drabber air. The building might have been fashionable in the decades before, but now trash strewed the sidewalk out front and it was surrounded by other derelict buildings.

Bolan parked the Suburban and sat studying the place. It had taken him no more than thirty minutes to find the address, located in an area on par with Vorchek's.

Bolan found himself at odds with his feelings. Here he was, in America, driving through broken-down areas that might have been in some third-world slum. It angered him that such places could exist, that Americans were forced to live in deprived areas, fighting to survive and falling prey to the likes of Marchinski and Tsvetanov.

Blocks away from these dark and hopeless streets, the bright lights of the other America shone with relentless vigor. There money, prestige and the American dream could all be achieved with hard work and enterprise.

The Marchinski and Tsvetanov organizations stood in between. They profited from both ends of the spectrum. Regardless of status or wealth, the mobs reached out with greedy hands and took.

Bolan parked the Suburban. He checked the 93R under his jacket and the Cold Steel Tanto knife sheathed on his belt. The shabby street was deserted except for a few drifting figures. Down the side of the target building he saw a couple of SUVs. Bolan slipped out of the Suburban and keyed the lock before he headed for the drug house.

He pushed through the weathered boards of the fence and as he neared the entrance, he saw dark figures detach from the parked cars. They sauntered in his direction. Self-styled hardmen who imagined they owned the streets.

"What do you want, asshole?"

The accent was harsh. The tone guttural. The pair wore smart, casual clothes and their jackets did not hide the bulge of the handguns they carried.

"Asked you what you want," the leader said again.

He was louder this time, and he thrust his face close to Bolan's.

"I heard you the first time," Bolan said.

"You messin' with me?"

The man slid his hand under his jacket, fingers curling around the butt of his holstered gun.

"No," Bolan said. "This is messing with you…"

He slammed his boot into the man's testicles. Extremely hard. The leader gave a yell, clutching at his body and folding forward. Bolan had already pulled out the Beretta and fisted it into the face of the second man—a crippling blow that dropped him to the sidewalk, blood streaming from the deep gash in his forehead.

The lead man was still functioning, after a fashion. He clutched his groin with one hand and clawed his handgun out from under his coat. Bolan turned to face him, thrust the muzzle of the Beretta into his chest and pulled the trigger. The Parabellum slug cored in and ended the man's actions. Bolan's hand flicked the Beretta, and he put a slug in the second man's skull.

The Executioner went into the building and started down a trash-strewn passage. At the far end, light showed from a partly open door. Bolan went directly to it.

He heard raised voices and someone shouting orders—something about an incoming delivery.

And then a man said clearly, "Go see what the hell is going on."

The door swung open and light spilled out into the passage. A man came out the door, straight at Bolan. He had an auto pistol in one hand, and he tracked it in Bolan's direction.

Bolan flicked the selector, and the 93R burned a triple 9 mm package that caught the gunman in the chest and bounced him off the wall, then pitched him facedown on the floor. Bolan went in through the open door, swerving to one side as a figure came at him, swinging a baseball bat. The bat missed, slamming against the door frame with a metallic sound. An aluminum bat, Bolan thought. Light but deadly if it struck human flesh.

Bolan continued to move forward, driving his right foot in a solid blow to the bat-wielding man's groin. Before the man could recover, Bolan turned about. He snatched the bat from the man's hands, reversed it and delivered his own strike. Bolan laid the bat alongside the man's jaw, dislocating the joint and opening a bloody gash in the yielding flesh. As the man fell back, Bolan swung again, the aluminum weapon crunching down across the guy's skull. The dealer went to his knees, then fell onto his face.

Bolan, the bat in his left hand, flicked the Beretta's selector to single-shot again to conserve ammunition. He tracked the pistol across the room. On the far side of the long table dominating the space, a man in a flowered shirt was racking the slide of a 9 mm Uzi. That was his first and last mistake of the day. Bolan sent a direct message from the 93R—a 9 mm slug that plowed a hole between the man's eyes and took him out of the game.

As the gunman fell out of sight, Bolan sensed a rush of movement to his left. He dropped to a crouch as a well-suited man came into view, burning a clip of bullets from an SMG. Bolan heard the slugs hammer the wall behind him. Down low he could see the shooter's trousered legs. He angled the Beretta and triggered a volley of shots that punched through the guy's pants and into his shins. The man dropped, and Bolan hit him with a second pair of slugs that jolted his head back.

A skinny man in black ran for the far exit, his long hair streaming behind him. Bolan followed and caught him before he reached the door. The baseball bat swung in a looping arc and cracked across the guy's right side, over his ribs. The man squealed and clapped his hands to his injured side, sucking air into his lungs. Bolan dropped the bat and caught hold of the long hair. He yanked back and the skinny man backpedaled. Bolan swung him round, released him and the man reeled out of control. He collided with the edge of the long table, scattering hundreds of dollars worth of cocaine to the floor.

Stepping up behind him, Bolan placed a big hand against the back of the man's skull and slammed him facedown on the table. There was a crunch as his nose was broken and twin streams of bright blood spurted from his nostrils.

"I have your attention now?" Bolan asked.

The skinny man, clutching blood-streaked hands to his nose, turned around and stared at the Executioner. Despite the blinding pain, he took note of the Beretta in Bolan's hand.

"Attention?" Bolan repeated.

Skinny nodded. He wasn't going to do anything that might increase the guy's anger.

"Yeah."

"Marchinski is in big trouble," Bolan said. "He's going to lose all this. And you're going to be his fall guy."

"I only work here," Skinny moaned.

The big pistol rose until it filled Skinny's eye line.

"Do the crime. Do the time."

"You shot Dom and Klein. You cracked Cook's skull." Skinny remembered his own hurt. "And you busted my damn nose."

"The point being?"

"I can have you up on assault charges."

"I like a guy with a sense of irony," Bolan said. "You sell drugs, deal in misery, but you figure you've been hard done by."

"I want my lawyer."

Bolan shook his head. "It doesn't work that way with me. I'm not a cop. Not any kind of law."

Skinny spat blood and blinked tears of pain from his eyes.

"So who are you?"

"Right now I'm the guy asking questions you'd better have some answers to."

"Or what? You're going to shoot me, too?"

"A distinct possibility. I don't like leaving talking witnesses around."

Skinny glanced down at the blood soaking his shirt-front.

"You could have asked without smashing my damn nose."

"It's a failing I have. Direct action always draws someone's attention."

"Do I get any second chances?"

"Give me answers, and it could be considered," Bolan said.

"Jesus, you make a guy work hard."

"I heard you talking about a delivery going down soon. Where and when?"

"What? You come in here and smash the place up, and now you want me to give you information for free?"

"There's a price," Bolan said. "Tell me what I need to know and I'll let you stay alive. One-time offer."

"I give you anything and my life won't be worth squat. The people I work for don't appreciate getting sold out."

"Your choice. Look at it this way. If you're dead, it won't matter at all. You have to weigh up the odds."

Skinny managed a wheezy laugh. He put his head back to help stop the flow of blood from his broken nose.

"Anyone ever tell you what a cold bastard you are?"

"Lots of people. All the time."

"Son of a bitch," Skinny said. "You would shoot me if I didn't play along. Right?"

"Another failing. I have this compulsion to get rid

of people like you and your drug buddies. I don't see what use you are in the world. If you need to confirm that, ask your late buddy, Vorchek. I just left him back at his place."

The sentiment stopped Skinny cold. He realized the man wasn't playing games. All it took was a glance into those ice-chipped blue eyes to know he was in earnest. For the first time in his life, Skinny was aware of being in the presence of death. The notion scared him more than anything had ever done before.

"What do I tell you?"

"When and where."

Skinny furnished the details and Bolan committed them to memory. A glance at his watch told him he still had time to make the rendezvous.

"Drugs have been transported up from the border. It's a regular run—twice a month. They come from a Mexican outfit we've been dealing with for a couple of years. The Campos syndicate out of Sinaloa. Drugs come across the border and they're sent up here through a number of contacts."

"This gas station?"

"It's been shut down a long time, so now it's kind of a halfway house. It's off the main highway—got by-passed when the new interstate was built."

Bolan evaluated the information. If he could make an intercept and deal out the players, both the Marchinski mob and the Mexican syndicate would suffer. He knew it wouldn't put a permanent end to their dealing, but at least both sides would suffer the indignity of having a deal interrupted and cash lost.

Skinny wiped the drying blood from his face.

"That pay my tab?"

Bolan holstered the Beretta. He saw relief wash over

Skinny's face. Bolan allowed him a moment before he moved in. His clenched fists landed powerful blows to the man's face. Skinny slumped to the floor unconscious. Bolan reached into his pocket and withdrew plastic ties. He secured the man's ankles and wrists, then used more ties to fasten him to the steel leg of a desk, which was heavy and bolted to the concrete floor. It would keep the man in place until someone came for him.

As he left the building, Bolan made another call to Stony Man and gave them the details on the drug house. Brognola could inform the local P.D. and get them to drop by.

Skinny would be angry when he was placed under arrest, but at least he would still be alive. Bolan had given his word on that.

FOLLOWING SKINNY'S INSTRUCTIONS, Bolan left the interstate, taking the slip road that would deliver him to the derelict gas station. After twenty miles, Bolan pulled off the single-lane road. He parked and turned off the engine. When he glanced at his watch, he saw he was well ahead of the prearranged meet. It would be dark in a couple of hours.

Bolan concealed the Suburban off the road, then donned his gear and made his way to the gas station, hiding in the collection of scavenged vehicles and rusting auto parts.

The first vehicle showed up on time, turning off the road to park on the empty forecourt of the gas station. It was a well-used 4x4 pickup. The open rear held an assortment of salvaged auto parts. The vehicle itself was dirty and streaked with rust, but the engine sounded smooth and healthy. There were three men in the vehicle. Two up front, the third in the crew seat behind them. They were all clad in scruffy work clothes, with oily ball caps on their heads. Once the vehicle stopped, the third man slipped out of the cab and made his way out of sight down the far side of the station building. The pair stayed put.

A quarter of an hour later, a second vehicle rolled into sight. It slowed as it passed the gas station, continued on for a couple of hundred yards, then made a leisurely turnabout and approached again. This time it made a right into the station and swung to a stop after angling to face the exit.

This one was a large SUV—a top-line model with gleaming silver paintwork and big wheels. The powerful engine under the hood barely broke the silence.

Three men climbed out of the vehicle. One immediately broke away from the group and headed across the forecourt. He carried a stubby SMG in his hands. The gunman walked out of sight down the same side of the building the first man had gone.

Both groups met, exchanging greetings and shaking hands. One of the newcomers opened the tailgate of the silver SUV. He pulled out metal toolboxes and placed them on the ground, then reached in deeper to slide out sealed, solid blocks of what Bolan assumed was the drug consignment. There was a brief delay while one of the receiving team dug the tip of a lock knife into one of the packs, drew out a small sample and checked it. The quick taste test satisfied him and he gave a nod.

Bolan watched as six packs were transferred from the truck to the SUV. The operation was repeated, with another half-dozen packages taken from the opposite side of the pickup truck.

He had just witnessed a fortune in illicit drugs being

handed over, and by the time the Marchinskis had cut and packaged the drugs, their value would be tripled. More profit for them as they supplied their customers, regardless of the end results.

Not this time.

Bolan eased the 93R from the shoulder holster and stepped out from cover.

His attention was attracted by a flicker of movement on his right. Bolan showed no outward sign that he'd seen anything, but he could distinguish the shape of a man coming toward his rear. Sunlight stroked the metal of the SMG the man carried. One of the two spotters who'd stationed themselves down the side of the building. The man had been doing his job—circling the building to check the area—and he'd spotted Bolan as he cleared the junk pile. The man had slipped into view as he'd stepped out from behind the building, moving slow and steady as he eased himself into position behind Bolan, his SMG rising.

Bolan dropped to a crouch.

He turned about to face the gunman.

The 93R came online, Bolan's finger stroking the light trigger, and the Beretta sent out its triple burst. The three 9 mm slugs hit the guy in the chest, over the heart. He stepped back, left hand slapping against the wounds. His knees buckled and he dropped, then fell facedown.

Bolan jammed the 93R into its holster and cradled the Uzi in his hands, turning it in the direction of the crew from the pickup. They had been replacing the toolboxes, and by the time they reached for their guns Bolan was taking them down by sweeping the weapon across their crouching bodies. Nine millimeter slugs punched home and dropped the pair in bloody sprawls.

The crackle of an SMG drew Bolan's attention to the second concealed shooter as he emerged from the cover of the building, firing on the move and sending a vicious spray of shots in Bolan's general direction.

Bolan felt a hot slice of pain across his right hip as one of the shots reached him. The Executioner took long strides, and he dove forward, skidding across the concrete and rolling under the high chassis of the pickup truck.

The shooter had already moved alongside the truck. Bolan saw his pounding boots as he came into sight. The Executioner hauled the Uzi into position and raked the shooter's lower legs with a sustained burst from the SMG. The man's scream was high and loud as the 9 mm slug ripped into his calves, shredding his pants and savaging flesh and bone. He dropped to his knees, clutching at his damaged limbs, and for a second he stared into the muzzle of Bolan's Uzi. Then Bolan fired and the volley blew the man's face and skull apart.

Bolan rolled clear of the pickup truck, pushing to his feet and turning to face the team from the SUV.

They had reacted to Bolan's assault by pushing the last of the packages into the SUV's trunk and slamming the tailgate door shut.

One headed for the driver's door.

The other turned about to confront Bolan, yanking a handgun from under his jacket.

It was too little, too late.

Bolan fired a hard burst and saw the man jerk as the 9 mms hit him high in the torso. They were likely not killing shots, but the man was hit hard enough to stumble back, his shoulder scraping the side of the SUV. He threw out one hand to steady himself, and that was when Bolan fired again. He had taken a couple of seconds to steady his aim, and this time he acquired his target fully. The slugs cored into the man's heart and he went down in a flurry of arms and legs, facedown, the handgun slipping free and clattering across the ground.

The sound of a powerful motor reached Bolan's ears. He cleared the 4x4 and moved forward as the silver SUV surged ahead, tires squealing for purchase as the driver slammed the pedal to the boards.

Bolan raised the Uzi as he ran toward the vehicle, lining up on the SUV's left front wheel. He triggered a pair of short bursts and saw fragments of black rubber erupt from the spinning tire. It blew with a soft sound, the wheel dropping onto the alloy rim. Still moving, Bolan fired into the rear tire and saw it deflate. The driver kept his foot on the gas pedal and the heavy vehicle sped across the concrete forecourt. He wrenched the steering wheel to the right as the SUV hit the road. It lurched to one side, wheels digging into the road surface. The powerful engine pushed the vehicle forward as the man kept his foot on the gas pedal, but the SUV was swerving from side to side.

Bolan never knew what caused the driver to suddenly slam on his brakes, trying to haul the heavy steering around. The result was the SUV dipping to the left, the weight transferring to the tireless wheels. The sheer bulk of the vehicle added to the effect, and Bolan saw the SUV lean sideways, reach the critical angle and tip over, crashing down hard onto its roof, the wheels still spinning. The motor roared until it choked and fell silent. Window glass was sprayed across the road surface.

Bolan circled around and approached the driver's door. The impact had sprung it open, the driver hanging partway out. He stared up at Bolan as the tall figure stepped into view. Blood was streaked across his face from a deep scalp wound.

"I think I broke my legs," the guy moaned. "And my arm."

Bolan let the Uzi hang by its strap and pulled out the 93R again.

"You going to help me out?"

"Give me a good reason why I should."

"I'm hurt, you son of a bitch."

"Aggressive language isn't about to help your case."

"You know who you're messing with? Sabaroff will rip out your heart."

"That's the man standing in for Leo Marchinski. Am I right?"

"So?"

"Not making much of an impression," Bolan said.

"Sabaroff is…"

Bolan allowed a thin smile to show. "Sabaroff's not here," he said. "You are. He can yell and stamp and throw his toys all he wants. It isn't going to prevent what'll happen to you."

The guy stared at Bolan, his face paling as he picked up a familiar smell.

Bolan had noticed, as well.

Gasoline.

Fuel was creeping out from beneath the SUV's crumpled hood, turning to vapor as it ran over hot engine components.

"I can't stay in here," the man said. "This thing could burn."

Bolan holstered the Beretta again, realizing he was in no danger from the driver. He made no move to help the man.

"My legs," the guy moaned. "My arm. They're broken. I can't move them."

"You told me that already."

The man was silent for a moment. He tried to move and groaned.

"Hurts, huh?"

"Damn right it does."

"You guys are all the same," Bolan said. "You play tough when it's time to terrorize your victims. But when it's your turn, you start sniveling."

"You'd stand there and let me burn?"

"Easily."

The odor of leaking gasoline increased and the man gave a half sob, his head drooping.

"Get me out," he whimpered. "Jesus, it hurts bad."

"It's time to pay."

"What?"

"My help. It's going to cost you."

"You miserable bastard. You think I carry a roll of bills in my pocket?"

"Information. Give me something useful."

"So you can carry it back to Tsvetanov? Sabaroff doesn't like snitches. If I do that, I'm toast."

"Not your best choice of words right now."

"Just help me."

"I heard the Marchinskis have gone into kidnapping. Tsvetanov would be interested in what that's all about."

"It's— Jesus, there's fire in here."

Bolan saw flames creeping along the exposed underside of the SUV from the exterior fuel line. Fingers of fire were trailing across the interior floor. Gasoline seeped through the fractured metal shell, and burning fuel dripped onto the injured man. He let out a terrified scream.

"Get me out!"

"Let's trade. A name first. A contact. Now."

"Damn it! Keppler—Jason Keppler… The lawyer… Get me…"

As Bolan breathed in, he noticed a higher concentration of gasoline coming from the rear of the SUV—where the fuel tank was located. He turned and saw the wet shine of gas running from under the rear seat… spilling down and spreading.

The man became hysterical, his voice rising in a high, shivering scream. He thrust his uninjured arm at Bolan.

"Get me out!"

Bolan caught hold of his wrist. He gripped with both hands and started to drag the screaming man from the overturned car.

Above the yells, Bolan heard a rising, sucking swell of sound. The pooling gasoline had ignited, flames racing across the interior…

Bolan knew how fast ignited gasoline could gather momentum. He knew his own life was in jeopardy. He maintained his grip and felt the injured man sliding out from the car.

The fire blew without warning. It filled the interior, heat radiating from the open door and hitting Bolan. He made a final effort to drag the screaming man clear.

Bolan felt his grip slide on the man's sweaty wrist and he turned his body to the side—away from the open door—as flames burst from the gap. In a moment, he was caught by the blast. He threw up his arms to cover his head as the surge of energy created by the fireball threw him aside. Bolan hit the ground on his left shoulder, letting his own momentum carry him away from the center of the burst. The hungry roar of the fireball filled his ears. Bolan kept moving in the fragment of time allowed, rolling his curled body away from the flames. The solid bulk of the SUV's body shielded him from the full surge.

The open driver's door had allowed the fireball an escape. That simple fact had prevented a full-on explosion that might have increased the overall strength of the blast.

Bolan ended up sprawled on the tarmac, facedown and breathing in smoke. He had the presence of mind to drag himself farther away, eyes streaming and lungs coughing up the acrid fumes. As soon as he was able, Bolan pushed to his feet, moving clear until he was able to turn and take in the scene.

He saw the body first—stretched out only a couple of feet from the SUV. Bolan didn't need to move any closer to know there was nothing he could do for the man. The surge of flame from the inside of the vehicle had engulfed the man's body and turned it into a charred corpse. His clothing had been partially burned away, the flesh beneath shriveled and blistered. The man's fractured legs were visible, and the splintered bones lay exposed where the ends had burst through the charred flesh. There was little left resembling a human face where it lay turned in Bolan's direction. Bolan walked slowly back to his SUV. He took out his cell and punched in the Stony Man number.

Brognola answered, his voice expressing his concern.

"Hey, Striker. We were worried when you hadn't called."

"It's been one of those days," Bolan said.

"You follow that lead?"

"Strike more of the Marchinski crew off the list."

"Did any useful information come out?" Brognola asked.

"Have Aaron check a name for me. Jason Keppler. I need to know where he stands on the Marchinski ladder. Might be a lead to where Abby Mason is. No guarantees, but I need to follow it through."

"I'll have the cyber team track him down. You sure you're okay? You sound hoarse."

"Things got a little hot here," Bolan said. "I'm fine."

"You wouldn't tell me if things weren't fine," Brognola pointed out.

"How's Mason doing?" Bolan asked, changing the subject.

"Working on his bluff. He's doing pretty good, too. Aaron has a tap on his phone so any calls he receives are monitored."

"I'll come back to you if anything develops."

"You watch yourself," Brognola said. "People here are concerned."

"I know. And thanks," Bolan said as he shut the call down.

Bolan slid behind the wheel, started his SUV and drove away from the area. He was able to see the smoke rising from the smoldering vehicle in his rearview mirror for some time. The fire would do no good to the drugs stored in the blazing SUV. A plus as far as Bolan was concerned.

When he'd finally got back to the motel, Bolan parked and went inside his unit, locking the door behind him.

He took off his jacket, noting the heavy scorch marks. The thick leather had most likely stopped him from receiving burns down his back. He stripped off the rest of his clothes and made his way to the bathroom.

Bolan turned on the shower and stood under the warm water, soaping himself to remove the smoky taint. He repeated the process a couple of times before he felt satisfied.

Wrapped in the motel bathrobe, Bolan walked back into the bedroom and flicked on the kettle. He made a mug of coffee and stretched out on the bed, finally allowing his body to relax. He would wait and see what Stony Man came up with on Jason Keppler.

A lawyer, the man had said.

The guy who kept his employer's people out of jail and turned them back on the streets so they could return to business.

Marchinski's lawyer would be likely to advise him on all kinds of legal matters—including the risk involved in kidnapping Abby Mason.

In that case, he might be the very man Bolan needed to talk to.

15

Marchinski Residence

Lazlo Sabaroff had his eye on the throne.

Until now, he'd faithfully stood in the shadows while Leo ran things and Gregor played second fiddle. The younger Marchinski had responsibility for a number of minor operations that—in reality—ran themselves. In deference to Leo, the rank and file played along, allowing Gregor his moments of glory. Yet they held little respect for the man. Gregor was a bully, but Leo had always indulged him.

Sabaroff had observed this for a number of years, and his personal feelings for Gregor were well concealed. There would come a day when Sabaroff's true feelings might surface but in the interim, Sabaroff played the faithful lieutenant to Leo.

Lazlo Sabaroff had been at Leo Marchinski's side from the early days. They'd been friends for a long time but never true equals. Leo was the one who commanded. He had the physical and mental prowess, and he was a natural businessman. Leo could organize and plan without breaking a sweat, and he had the ability to draw people in and nurture them. Leo gave them hope and pride in their abilities. He also provided them with material goods and accommodation. It was sound management. Content workers were less liable to complain. Like any good employer, Leo Marchinski had his people covered by professional legal teams. If anyone had trouble with the law, there was always someone available to get them back on the streets quickly.

As the organization grew, Sabaroff had established his position as Leo's SIC. He learned the workings of the business operations, which allowed him to deal with minor events without involving Leo. He did this quietly, without any outward signs of doing so.

After all, Leo Marchinski had a streak of paranoia. He'd survived two attempted takeovers—one from a rival organization, the other from within the Marchinski mob. When these attempts had been discovered, Leo Marchinski had struck with chilling ferocity. Both rivals were dispatched swiftly—a warning to anyone contemplating similar moves.

So Sabaroff had watched and learned. His personal ambition did not wither, but it was concealed. He waited for an opportunity. When Leo was arrested and charged with the murder of Jake Bixby, Sabaroff's plans came closer to reality.

The sudden emergence of a threat from the Tsvetanov organization had come as a shock. There had always been a rivalry between the groups, an occasional skirmish when boundaries were crossed. Now, with Leo out of the picture, it appeared Drago Tsvetanov was doing more than simply flexing his muscles.

The clashes were becoming stronger. There were dead on both sides and valuable merchandise had been destroyed.

Something was not quite right.

Some of these strikes could not have been orchestrated by either group. Unless there was a third party involved—someone playing the two sides against each other.

16

New York City

The office of Jason Keppler, Attorney at Law, was located on the third floor of a high-rise building. The ultramodern reception area featured pale wood floors and gleaming steel furniture. A pair of large desks faced each other, and two young women peered at Bolan over slim computer monitors.

Mack Bolan wore a dark suit, pale cream shirt and a dark tie. His shoes were polished and so was the smile he offered the receptionists. He also wore steel-rimmed spectacles and a trimmed mustache. Disguises were not something Bolan used very often, but he'd decided to use a little distraction.

The women looked him over, impressed by his physique and his imposing height. Bolan paused, standing between the evenly spaced desks as he acknowledged each young woman in turn.

"Can we help?" they asked, almost in tandem, then laughed at the situation.

"I need a quick word with Mr. Keppler," Bolan said quietly, lifting the attaché case he was carrying.

"Do you have an appointment?" one of the women asked.

Bolan leaned slightly in her direction, his blue eyes warm.

"Do I really need one?"

The woman blushed. "Mr. Keppler doesn't see anyone without an appointment," she said. Her tone was almost apologetic. "You see…"

"I should have explained," Bolan said. "My business has to do with the Marchinski group. It's urgent. Mr. Sabaroff asked me to stop by."

Marchinski was obviously the magic word.

Both young women sat up straighter, and the one Bolan had spoken with reached for the intercom unit. She tapped her manicured finger on the appropriate button, leaning forward to speak.

"There's a gentleman here who needs to speak with you urgently. He's from Mr. Sabaroff."

Bolan heard a low reply. The receptionist offered a quick smile as she looked at Bolan.

"Mr. Keppler will be—"

The door to the main office opened. The man who stepped out was tall and lean. He had medium-blond, neatly cut hair, and his tanned face was relaxed. He wore a suit and shirt that must have set him back a considerable sum. He extended a long-fingered hand and beckoned Bolan to follow him into the office. Bolan couldn't fail to notice the watch on his wrist—a $40,000 Patek Philippe Nautilus featuring a stainless-steel casing with white-gold hour markings and an alligator-skin-embossed strap.

Business is obviously good, Bolan thought as he followed Keppler into his office.

If the reception area had been plush, Keppler's office outshone it easily.

Everything spoke of money—from the vast desk to

the cream leather chairs to the pair of wide, curving sofas that sat beside the wet bar. The pictures on the walls were that much more expensive than the ones outside. The computer on Keppler's desk was the same high-end brand as the ones outside, but the monitor was far larger.

Directly across from the door was a wide picture window that stretched from floor to ceiling. It offered an unmatched view of the city.

Bolan didn't allow the impressive layout to distract him. Keppler represented the Marchinskis—people who traded in drugs and pornography, who bought and sold vulnerable young women like livestock. This outwardly respectable lawyer helped to keep them free and clear.

Bolan squeezed his hand around the handle of his attaché case, his knuckles turning white as he fought the impulse to take Keppler down right there and then. Instead, the Executioner shut the heavy door, his left hand reaching behind him to quietly turn the internal lock.

"I wasn't expecting a visit from…"

Keppler's words trailed off as he saw the suppressed Beretta 93R Bolan had slipped from the attaché case. The muzzle rose and settled on Keppler's chest.

The tanned face became deathly pale. Keppler raised a hand to touch his mouth as if he'd already been hurt.

"No fuss, Keppler," Bolan said quietly. "No shouting. No screaming."

"Lazlo didn't send you."

Bolan's smile had no trace of humor as he paced across the thick carpet, the 93R held rock-steady. He placed the attaché case on the floor beside the desk.

"With a brain like yours, I can see why the Marchinskis hired you."

Keppler regained a little backbone. "Then you must

realize I know my job. You won't get away with whatever it is you're planning. I can have you thrown in jail for this."

"You think so? It'll be hard to do that if I shoot you before I leave."

"You can't just walk in and—"

"I'm pretty certain nobody told Harry Jigs that before they killed him."

"Jigs? Who's Harry Jigs?"

"Nice guy. Sold information. He was pretty low on the ladder—the kind of man you wouldn't notice if you passed him on the street. Keppler, don't insult me by pretending you never heard of him." Bolan's tone hardened, and the expression in his cold eyes made Keppler take a step back. "You've got guilt written all over your face."

"You have me all wrong," Keppler said. "I just represent Mr. Marchinski when he needs assistance on simple business deals."

"Which deals are those? His drug negotiations? Or the porn business? Stolen cars? You want me to recite the whole list of crimes you cover him for?"

"You can't walk in here and accuse me of anything like that."

Bolan raised his arm, aiming the Beretta at Keppler's face.

"This says I can. Right now, Keppler, all your legal arguments don't mean a thing. All I see is a man wallowing in the dirt, taking money to represent lowlife criminals. Marchinski muscle isn't going to get you out of this. Leopold is sitting in jail, waiting to go on trial for murder. His brother, Gregor, and Lazlo Sabaroff are running the family firm while he's away—still dealing, still watching the dollars roll in. They have their hands full. And let's not forget the problems they're having with the Tsvetanov organization."

"Is that who you work for? The Tsvetanovs? I should have guessed."

"Then you understand the position you're in—not a very enviable one. If I do work for Drago Tsvetanov, I might be here to put you out of your misery."

"Is there a way we can work this out?"

Bolan lowered the Beretta. He could see the gleam in Keppler's eyes. The man was thinking ahead, analyzing the situation, formulating a plan to extract himself from this predicament. He would come up with valid arguments, reasons why it would not be in Bolan's interest to kill him. After all, he would argue, as the legal arm of the Marchinski machine, he possessed valuable information. Keppler might be willing to save himself by turning his back on his current employer.

Bolan allowed Keppler his thinking time.

A thin sheen of sweat lay across Keppler's face. He raised a slow hand to flick at the moisture forming in the corner of an eye.

"Can I get a drink?" he asked.

Bolan nodded in the direction of the wet bar and Keppler edged toward it. He took a heavy tumbler and produced a bottle of Jim Beam from the shelf. The hand pouring the whiskey shook noticeably. When Keppler raised the tumbler to his lips, he had to grip it in both hands. He swallowed quickly then poured himself a second glass.

"Make that the last," Bolan said. "I need you with a clear mind."

"That damned gun is making me nervous. I don't like guns. Never have."

"Working for Leopold Marchinski you should be

used to them. They're part of his business, a business that creates a great deal of money."

"Is that what this is about? Money?" Keppler smiled nervously. "Perhaps we need to talk about that."

"Could be."

Keppler warmed to the slight encouragement.

"I'm beginning to see a picture here. Let me make a considered guess. You don't seem the type who would be on Tsvetanov's regular payroll. You're a contractor, brought in as an enforcer. Tsvetanov must be paying you to harass Marchinski's people and hit his business interests while Leopold is out of the picture."

"And if that were true?" Bolan said.

"There's always the chance for a better offer…" Keppler took a hasty gulp of whiskey. "Happens all the time. Man has to look out for himself. New deals can be made—better deals." Keppler smiled. "I see you as a smart man with an eye to the future—a money-rich future."

Bolan allowed the Beretta's muzzle to drop a couple of inches. He saw the shine of relief in Keppler's eyes; the man was relaxing a little.

"You suggesting some kind of deal?"

Keppler swallowed more of his whiskey, cleared his throat.

"We could work something out. Leo Marchinski has a reputation as a good employer. He treats his people well."

Bolan made a point of gazing around the office.

"I can see that. Pretty sharp place you have."

"Like I said. Marchinski pays for the best."

The Beretta was pointing at the floor now.

"I hope he's getting his money's worth these days."

"Meaning?"

"The man is behind bars and likely looking at a hell of a stretch."

"Wheels are in motion."

"Legal wheels? Let's hope they stay on track. From what I've been hearing, Leopold Marchinski was caught in the act. You're a good lawyer, Keppler, but even you're going to find it hard to talk your client free."

"You seem to know a lot."

"In my line of work, keeping up with events is important."

Bolan made a show of returning the Beretta to his shoulder holster, smoothing the line of his suit jacket to conceal the weapon.

Keppler stared down at the amber liquid in his tumbler and swirled it around.

"I'm wondering how much you know that you aren't telling me."

"I do my homework, counselor. I like to know what I'm walking in on before I commit."

"You think you know everything about Marchinski's organization?"

"I can see it's struggling to pull Leopold Marchinski out of a cell—so desperate, it paints a target on itself by snatching the prosecutor's kid."

Keppler didn't answer, but Bolan didn't miss the way his face paled at the mention of Abby Mason.

"Don't get me wrong. It's a good play. Let's hope it comes off. Kidnapping is a risky deal and from where I'm standing, you're just as guilty."

"Is that a threat?"

"Hell, no. It's just that law-enforcement agencies have a tendency to get all righteous about kidnapping—especially kids. But being a qualified lawyer, I'm sure you advised your client against it."

"Of course I did. I had to make him realize what he was getting into here."

"And Leo just sat back and ignored what you said."

"He said to go ahead and do it."

"The act of a desperate man."

Keppler made no comment.

"What about Sabaroff? Was he on board?"

"He'll be loyal as long as the possibility exists that Leo might get away with the scheme. If Sabaroff realizes it isn't going to happen, he'll be the first in line for the king's seat."

"You let him know it's a losing scheme?"

"If you knew Sabaroff, you'd realize he doesn't take kindly to being lectured. He's a hard man. That's why he's Leo Marchinski's top aide. Gregor may be Leo's brother, but he doesn't have the Marchinski touch. Sabaroff is the guiding hand." Keppler took a breath. "If Leo doesn't get out of prison, the new boss won't be Gregor. Sabaroff will step in without hesitation."

Bolan digested the statement.

If it was true, Sabaroff would be directing operations, with Gregor doing low-level stuff just to maintain the Marchinski image.

"Sabaroff takes over if Leo falls," Bolan said. "Betrayed by his closest lieutenant. It sounds very Shakespearian."

"I learned early on that looking out for yourself is more important than misguided loyalty. Leo had a good run, but things come to an end, and if you take your eye off the ball…"

"You could go down with the sinking ship."

"Unless you switch sides before it happens." Keppler managed a slight shrug of his expensively clothed shoulders. "A change of management."

"Counselor, you give new meaning to the phrase *keeping it in the family*."

"I've seen Leo turn on people who've been with him for a long time. Jake Bixby was an employee for years and Leo killed him without turning a hair. When Leo told me about kidnapping Larry Mason's daughter, I knew he was making another mistake. I said I wasn't sure it would work, but that was as far as I went. It wouldn't have been wise to tell Leo Marchinski he was doing something stupid. Hell, I thought about it, but then I recalled that baseball bat with Bixby's brains on it." Keppler forced a smile. "I realized how easily that could happen to me."

"So you stepped back and watched. Let the game play out."

"In a manner of speaking. I had to let the dust settle so I could make a calculated choice."

"Leo or Sabaroff."

"I enjoy my life," Keppler said. "A change in leadership would let me maintain my lifestyle. If that makes me cynical, I can live with it."

"With that in mind, I won't be turning my back on you any time soon."

"Should I care? You haven't come to my office out of charity. Let's say I offered you information that might advance your cause. Would you be interested?"

"Go on."

"If the girl was taken away from where she's being held, Leo would lose his influence over Mason."

"And what's in it for me?"

"Whatever you want—success for your employer, a hit against the Marchinski organization, a way in if that's what you wanted."

Bolan could see why Keppler was a lawyer. The man

talked the talk. He was also a two-faced wheeler-dealer, seizing the opportunity that had presented itself. In this instance, he was ready to cast aside any loyalty he had for Leo Marchinski. Keppler was siding with the next in line and preparing to consolidate his own position.

Bolan experienced a sense of loathing for this man. "Where's the girl?"

Jason Keppler stared at Bolan, his mind working quickly. "Are you…?"

"Taking you up on your offer? Keppler, I didn't come here to check your water cooler. Don't dance around. If we're going to do this, make it happen."

Keppler hesitated for a few seconds more then turned and moved behind his desk. He drew a scratch pad to him and picked up a pen, quickly writing. He tore off the top sheet of paper and handed it to Bolan.

The figures on the pad were sat-nav coordinates. Underneath was a cell phone number.

Bolan folded the paper and slid it into a pocket.

"Call me," Keppler said.

"You'll be hearing from me," Bolan replied.

He meant it. Not in the way Keppler expected, but they would be meeting again.

17

Appalachians

The Marchinski safe house was located in wooded hills off the main highway, making it isolated and easy to defend. Sitting close to a ragged outcrop of rock, with a steep fall protecting its eastern boundary, the safe house had open ground on the other three sides. Behind the low spread of the house, in the distance, rugged, timbered hills provided a natural backdrop.

Bolan had driven for almost four hours, leaving the city at dawn. Now he lay prone, studying the layout, assessing the odds, knowing he would eventually have to make his move. The Executioner had been in place for nearly two hours, concealed by his camouflage gear and the spread of vegetation. His ordnance was in the backpack he wore over his shoulders. The big Desert Eagle was holstered at his side, and he wore his 93R in its shoulder rig. A Cold Steel Tanto knife was sheathed and strapped to his thigh.

Bolan's silent observation had provided some intel, but not as much as he would've liked.

He'd spotted two parked 4x4s, and a couple of guards making loose circuits of the property. From the way they moved and the way they were dressed, Bolan knew these were city boys—reluctant soldiers working well out of their comfort zone—but he didn't dismiss them. Any man carrying an SMG was dangerous.

Bolan hadn't been able to get an accurate count of the guards inside, despite having a powerful pair of compact binoculars. The windows allowed him some access to the interior, but the ground was at a lower point than the house. It restricted his viewing angle.

He was left with little data on the number of people inside, and he wasn't too happy about that. But there was nothing he could do about it, so Bolan concentrated on what he could see.

Two parked vehicles.

A pair of guards outside.

Beyond the house, he saw a squat structure, stone built with a slightly pitched roof and a metal chimney with a capped vent. Bolan guessed that was the generator housing. Electricity wouldn't be piped into such a remote spot, so the house would have its own power supply. When Bolan had scanned the outhouse, he spotted a medium-sized fuel tank jutting out from behind it. All very self-sufficient.

Bolan drew away from his surveillance spot and checked his watch. Late morning. He would have preferred a night assault, but Bolan needed to move fast. The sooner he pulled Abby out of the hands of the Marchinskis, the better he would feel.

He had set up both crews—the Marchinskis and Tsvetanovs—for a final showdown. But the conflict wouldn't distract the Marchinskis for long. Patience would evaporate quickly if Larry Mason failed to keep his side of the bargain—uneven though it was.

If Mason kept Gregor Marchinski and Lazlo Sabaroff waiting, there could be dire consequences for Abby.

Bolan knew the kind of people he was dealing with. Life had little meaning to them—even that of a child. The Marchinskis enslaved hapless young women and sold illicit goods and drugs—death was a by-product of their business…death from overdosing and from the crime that followed when an addict stole to feed the habit. Leo Marchinski had little conscience. He focused on the vast amounts of money his business created rather than the suffering he caused.

So why would the death of a single child concern him?

Bolan knew the answer.

It wouldn't.

Marchinski wanted his freedom, and he would do anything to achieve it. His crew would follow his orders, and if the order came to take a young life, then it would be obeyed.

That realization settled any doubts Bolan had.

He had his objective.

Free Abby and deal out Bolan-style justice to the ones holding her.

He was not their judge.

Not their jury.

He was their Executioner.

Bolan opened the backpack and drew out a 9 mm Uzi. He also extracted a matte black Gemtech Mossad-II suppressor. The attachment weighed 12 ounces and was nearly eleven inches long. Bolan unscrewed the existing barrel-retaining ring and screwed the Gemtech suppressor into place. He snapped in a 32-round magazine. Laying the Uzi aside, Bolan took out a combat harness, quickly pulling it on. The loaded pouches held extra magazines for his weapons—the Uzi, the 93R and the Desert Eagle on his hip. The backpack was pushed out of sight beneath tangled foliage.

Bolan didn't want to risk hurting Abby Mason, so he left behind the fragmentation and stun grenades in his ordnance bag. He would depend on the controllable power of conventional weapons. That might leave him with reduced capability, but it was something he had to accept. If Abby had not been inside the building, Bolan could have gone in on a full assault, blitzing through with little regard for anything but his own life, but today Abby's safety was his priority.

Bolan checked both handguns and reholstered them. He was as ready as the situation would allow.

The Executioner looped the Uzi's strap over his head and allowed the weapon to hang free. His initial assault would be on the two sentries. He needed to eliminate them quietly, without alerting the people inside the house.

Bolan silently skirted the house, under cover of the treeline until he reached the angled slope backing the building. From where he crouched, Bolan saw the rear of the house above him.

The slope held a scattering of brush and stunted trees. Bolan studied the area for a few minutes, deciding on his best path, before he started to work his way up the incline. He moved steadily, using the foliage as cover and pausing frequently to make sure he was still clear. It took him twenty minutes of careful maneuvering before he reached the top of the slope.

Bolan edged forward, keeping the bulk of the house's rear wall above him. There was a single wide window in the back wall, but no one could spot him from that angle.

Edging around the rear wall, Bolan checked the side

of the house. A pair of large windows were cut into this section—one at the back, the second closer to the front. Someone checking from those windows could easily spot suspicious movement.

Bolan crouched and edged his way along the wall, pressed in against the rough natural stone. He was only feet away from the front corner when he heard the tread of footsteps on the gritty earth.

It had to be one of the sentries.

The way the man moved told Bolan he was in no hurry to complete his patrol. Bolan could also smell tobacco smoke. Staying low—back pressed hard against the stone wall—he reached down, removed the combat knife from its sheath and held it in his right hand.

The steps became louder.

Closer.

The sentry appeared. He was half turned away, staring out toward the distant treeline. Smoke trailed from the cigarette between his lips. He took a couple of steps, bringing himself to the apex of the corner.

Bolan had no way of knowing whether the second man was in the line of sight. His chance had come, and if he hesitated too long, his target might turn about and step beyond reach.

Bolan grabbed the man's coat with his left hand. Before the sentry could brace himself, Bolan hauled him close, catching him off balance. The Executioner swung the man around and slammed him against the stone wall. The sentry gasped under the impact, the cigarette flying from his lips.

Bolan had seconds to act. The man was going to yell—that was a given—and Bolan didn't want him to warn the other guard. The Executioner raised the Tanto's gleaming blade and cut across the exposed throat, right to left, the ultra sharp steel biting in deep. It severed everything in its path—flesh and muscle and blood carriers. The sentry's eyes widened in total shock. An SMG slipped from his grip and hit the ground as the man reached up to clutch at his throat, blood already swelling from the wound. It spurted between his fingers, spilling down his shirtfront, soaking the material.

Bolan had already stepped back to check the position of the second sentry. He was in time to see the man step into sight from around the far corner of the house.

One down, one to go.

Bolan heard a wet gurgle coming from the man, now on his knees and frantically trying to suck air into his lungs. Both hands at his throat were covered in blood. More was still bubbling between his fingers, spilling in a torrent to his waist. The man fell back against the wall, sliding to one side until he was on the ground, body going into spasms.

Slipping the knife back into its sheath, Bolan brought the Uzi into play.

Peering around the corner of the house, Bolan checked out the second sentry. The man was already moving in his direction. He didn't exhibit any signs of alarm. Most likely he figured his partner was checking the side of the house.

That would change when the first sentry failed to reappear. Bolan needed to move quickly, but the second man was moving past the house's main windows. If anyone looked out as Bolan took the sentry down, any surprise would be lost. He'd have to risk it.

The man was nearly twelve feet away. Bolan leaned around the corner, raised the Uzi and triggered a three-round burst that hammered the guy's chest, over his heart. The 9 mm slugs cored in and delivered a killing blow that toppled the startled sentry. He skidded and fell, hitting the ground hard, his body raising puffs of dust.

18

The moment he fired, Bolan cleared the corner of the building and sprinted for the stairs leading to the veranda and the front entrance. He hit the steps at a run then raised his left foot and slammed it against the door, just below the handle. The door burst open, splintered wood flying as the lock assembly was ripped from its housing.

Bolan stepped into a wide entrance hall, doors on either side. The Uzi scanned right and left. To Bolan's right, an open double door showed a large open-plan lounge.

An armed figure rushed forward, bringing up the stubby-barreled shotgun he was carrying. His erratic move meant his first and only shot went way off target. Bolan's follow-up Uzi burst ripped into the man's midsection. He folded forward so that Bolan's second burst took the top of his skull off in a mélange of blood and gray brain matter. The guy performed a nosedive to the floor.

Two others were already on the move. One grabbed a Benelli shotgun that was resting against a coffee table. The second man pushed up off a wide leather couch, hauling a stainless-steel auto pistol from a shoulder holster.

Bolan let the Uzi complete its swing in their direction, his finger already stroking back on the trigger. The hard-fired burst caught the shotgunner as he pulled the Benelli on track. He was hit high in the chest, the 9 mm slugs half turning him. The shotgun boomed loudly in the confines of the room, the 12-gauge shot hammering into the wall as the man fell back. He tangled with the coffee table and stumbled, going down with a heavy crash. Before the man hit the floor, Bolan had dropped to a crouch, targeting the second gunman as he cleared his pistol from its holster. The pistol cracked too soon, the slug clearing Bolan's head by a few feet. When the Uzi fired, the shots took a bloody chunk of flesh from the guy's throat, left side, and the resultant burst of blood misted the air. The man clasped his hand over the gory wound as he tried for a second shot at Bolan. The Executioner triggered another short burst that punched in through the man's torso and put him down.

Raised voices were coming from the far side of the lounge, where a doorway led to another room. Bolan heard pounding footsteps, and a shirtsleeved figure appeared, a pistol in his hand.

The man was tall and heavyset, with a mass of dark hair and a thick beard. He was closely followed by a second man, this one in a baggy T-shirt and jeans. The dark-haired man saw Bolan and threw a quick shot in his direction. The slug burned across Bolan's left upper arm, leaving a stinging wound.

The Uzi tracked in, Bolan triggering a series of 9 mm Parabellum bursts that hit the bearded guy and his partner, who had crowded in close. The bloody strikes had the desired effect and both shooters went down, lying still.

When Bolan scouted the area beyond the lounge, he

found the kitchen. Satisfied it was clear, he went back across the lounge and stepped into the front hall. Bolan crossed to check the doors on the far side, kicking each door open and making sure the rooms were empty.

That left the stairs leading to the upper floor. Partway up, a landing extended left and right. There was no easy way to reach the top, so Bolan made his approach fast, eyes scanning the empty landing.

Close to the top of the stairs, Bolan picked up a rustle of clothing coming from the right of the landing. An armed figure leaned out from behind the wall, pushing a handgun into view. Bolan swept the Uzi up and triggered a pair of hot bursts that ripped the shooter's hand apart in a welter of blood and lacerated flesh, the pistol dropping away from the ruined fingers. The guy let out a howl of terror as he saw his hand disintegrate. He clutched at his wrist, staring at the mangled wound in complete shock.

Bolan stepped in close, jamming the suppressor against the man's cheek.

"Where is she?"

The man failed to respond.

"Make it right," Bolan snapped. "The girl doesn't deserve this."

Tears filled the man's eyes as he turned to stare at Bolan. When the man saw the unforgiving expression on the Executioner's face, he pressed his shattered hand to his chest, covering the mutilated mess with his free one.

"Room to the left," he whispered.

"Alone?"

"One of our guys. And Gregor… He'll kill her."

Bolan kicked the fallen pistol through the bannister rail. It dropped to the floor below.

"What about me?" the man pleaded.

"What about you?" Bolan asked as he smashed the Uzu against the injured man's skull. As his victim collapsed to the floor, the Executioner headed across the landing.

19

The door was partway open, and Bolan picked up movement on the other side. He let the Uzi hang by the strap and took the Beretta from his shoulder rig. Bolan reached out with his left hand and gave the door a gentle push, enough so that it swung wide to show the room beyond.

Even though the room was large, it contained only a single bed and a couple of wooden chairs. The window was barred.

A shadow angled across the floor from Bolan's left. Boards creaked. In front of him was Gregor Marchinski. He was a younger, thinner version of his brother and there was a weakness in his pale features.

"Leave, or she's dead," Gregor said.

He held an auto pistol in his right hand, the muzzle touching the cheek of the nine-year-old girl he held tight against him.

Bolan had seen her face before—in the photo in Larry Mason's kitchen.

Abby Mason stared at Bolan, wide-eyed, yet showing defiance.

"Give it up, Marchinski. It's over," Bolan said quietly.

"I will kill her if you don't back off."

"Think this through, Gregor. Your brother isn't walking free. Killing the girl isn't going to change that. You pull that trigger and you'll be dead a second later. That is definite. I don't negotiate. I don't back down. Whatever bargaining power you might have had is finished. Leopold is still locked away, and he's going to do his time—no question there. If you carry this through, he won't have a brother on the outside. Your choice."

Bolan had remained outside the room. He knew the armed man behind the cover of the door was waiting for him to clear the opening so he could make his shot.

Bolan was able to peer through the gap between door and frame. He made out the arm and part of the man's body.

Gregor was not going to harm the girl. She was his one chance at walking from the house in one piece. As long as she was alive, she was a bargaining chip.

At that precise moment in time, all Bolan had to worry about was the man concealed by the door.

Bolan gripped the strap supporting the Uzi and lowered the weapon to the floor, pushing it aside with his foot.

"Time to negotiate," he said, directing his words at Gregor.

"Not with that gun in your hand."

Bolan lowered the Beretta a fraction. "This?"

A nervous tic edged Gregor's mouth.

Bolan tensed his muscles, preparing to make his move. He was going to have one shot at this.

He powered forward, his leg muscles thrusting him through the door. Bolan launched himself in a long dive, tucking in his left shoulder, arm extended, and executed a roll that threw him across the floor. As he landed, skimming the floor and twisting so his right hand curved around, the 93R tracked the dark shape of the shooter. The man had been caught off guard when Bolan came in low, and a burst of auto fire went high over Bolan's body, slamming into the far wall. The Beretta chugged out a triple burst that hit the man in the chest, kicking him back against the wall. The gunman lost his weapon, gripping his body as Bolan pushed to his feet, angling the Beretta and delivering a second burst of 9 mm slugs that dropped the would-be-shooter to the floor.

Bolan turned about, the Beretta picking up on Gregor, the barrel settling on his head.

"Don't convince yourself anyone else is coming to help. That was your last line of defense. There's no one left. So right now it's down to you, Gregor. Just you. What would your brother do? Is he the bigger man? The one who holds the reins? He left you to handle things and you messed up."

Gregor's expression changed. He took on the look of someone who knew he was failing badly but refused to accept his inadequacy. This was Gregor's chance to prove himself, to show he was his brother's equal.

"No. You're wrong. I can do this. I don't need any of them."

"Show me how. All I'm hearing is talk."

The hand holding the gun trembled slightly.

"You want this girl dead?" Gregor yelled.

"She's the only card left for you to play," Bolan said. "Without her, Leo definitely stays in jail. It's your decision, Gregor."

Bolan was watching Gregor closely, tracking the way the pistol jerked back and forth. Gregor Marchinski was close to losing it.

"Last chance, Gregor. Don't lose your only bargaining chip."

Sweat shone on Marchinski's face. He reached up with the hand holding the pistol to wipe the moisture streaming down into his eyes, stinging and obscuring his vision. It was a brief, foolish gesture that gave Bolan the window he needed.

And there was no hesitation. The Beretta's muzzle moved a fraction and Bolan shot Gregor. A head shot that put three slugs into Gregor Marchinski's skull. He jerked aside, the back of his skull blowing open. A bloody spray of brain and bone fragments hit the wall behind him.

Bolan had instantly stepped forward, left arm reaching out to encircle Abby Mason's slim form as she tried to pull away from Gregor. He snatched her clear and turned her away from Gregor's bloody corpse as the man dropped to the floor.

He made for the door, Abby clinging to him, her face buried against his side.

Bolan paused on the landing, long enough to refresh the Beretta with a new magazine. He recovered the Uzi. As they descended the stairs, Bolan scanned the lower floor. Nothing moved.

They exited the door and cut to the left, clearing the house and making for the spot inside the tree line where Bolan had stashed his backpack.

"I want you to stay close to me," he said.

Abby nodded, watching as he holstered the Beretta and fed a fresh mag into the Uzi's grip, cocking the weapon.

"Are you going to take me home?"

Bolan glanced at her. The girl's eyes were scanning his outfit and the weapons he carried.

"Your dad is waiting for you."

For the first time, a smiled edged her lips.

"Are you one of the good guys?"

"I try to be. My name is Matt Cooper. Nice to meet you, Abby Mason."

"There was a lot of shooting before you came to my room. Was that you?"

Bolan nodded. "Those men didn't want me to take you away. It got a little noisy."

"I took a look when we went down the stairs. I saw bodies. Did you shoot those men?"

Her question was direct, uttered with the frankness that only a child could deliver.

Bolan shrugged the bag across his back, tightening the carry straps.

"Yes," he said. "They wanted to stop me from taking you home."

"So that means you're a policeman."

"A kind of policeman."

"Is my dad okay?"

"Yes. He's been worried about you since those people took you away. He's missed you very much."

Bolan took her hand, feeling the girl's fingers grip his. They had only gone a few steps when she stopped, staring up at Bolan.

"They killed Nancy," she said. "They didn't have to do that. It was cruel."

"Sometimes people do cruel things, Abby, because they believe it's necessary to get what they want. It isn't. The men who did that to Nancy and took you were trying to force your dad to do something bad. But he refused and asked me to help."

"I want to go home, Matt. Take me home."

"We need to walk for a while to reach my car. You going to be okay?"

"Will there be other men looking for us?"

"I hope not. If anything does happen, just do whatever I tell you."

Abby nodded.

It took them a quarter of an hour to reach Bolan's SUV. He took the slim remote from the zip pocket in his pants and unlocked the doors. While Bolan slipped the backpack free, Abby scrambled into the vehicle and secured the seat belt. Bolan got behind the wheel and depressed the starter button. The deep growl of the SUV's motor sounded.

He took out the cell he'd placed in the glove box and contacted Stony Man. Brognola answered his call.

"And?" the big Fed asked.

"I have a young lady on the passenger seat who can't wait to see her dad."

Brognola's sigh of relief was expansive.

"Is she okay?"

"Ask her yourself," Bolan said and handed the cell to Abby. "It's your godfather."

"Hi, Uncle Hal. Yes, I'm okay. No, they didn't hurt me, but I got scared. They were not very nice people. I have a new friend now. His name is Matt. He's going to take me home to my dad. Matt made the bad guys let me go. Yes, it was scary. Lots of shooting, but Matt had to do that because they wouldn't let me go. I'll see you later." She thrust the cell at Bolan. "He wants you now."

"Uncle Hal," Bolan said.

"I'll be a long time living that one down," Brognola said.

"You will."

"There's no way I can say thank you enough. I don't have the right words."

"Just let her dad know we're on our way."

"That I can do. Take it easy, Striker. Come on home."

Bolan ended the call, put the SUV into Drive and headed for the main highway. He drove steadily over the rough track. Beside him, the girl sat silently staring out through the windshield. She turned to look at him, and Bolan sensed something on her mind.

"Should I call you Uncle Matt?"

Bolan smiled. "Whatever you choose, Abby."

"I think I'll just call you Matt. Calling you Uncle makes you sound old."

Bolan's smile broadened as he thought about Brognola's reaction to that statement.

20

The squeal of rubber made Bolan glance in the rear-view mirror. A pair of SUVs was coming up fast, one behind the other.

How the hell had they shown up so fast?

Someone must have made a call from the house once his presence had been known. It didn't take that much time to hit speed dial and call for help. Even while Bolan had been putting down the Marchinski crew, reinforcements had been on the way.

None of that mattered right now. Bolan had hostiles on his six and a child in the car...the one he'd promised to take away from the Marchinskis.

Bolan stepped on the gas. The chase vehicles increased their speed.

This was not about to go away.

"Is something wrong?" Abby asked. "You keep looking in the mirror. Is it because of those two cars following us?"

"Yes. It looks like some of the bad guys are here. Somehow they found out what happened back there."

"Oh. Matt, I think I know what happened. That man—Gregor—when he heard the shooting he made a call on his cell. I couldn't understand what he was saying because he spoke in a foreign language. It might have been Russian but I'm not sure. He sounded scared."

Bolan digested the words. He realized now why backup had arrived so fast. The Marchinski crew could have been maintaining an arm's-length watch over the hideout. Close but not too close in case their presence became suspect. Bolan's incursion had been missed until he encountered resistance, and Gregor's call had brought the cavalry on the double. He suspected the additional watch had been mounted since he'd started stirring up trouble between the Marchinskis and Tsvetanovs. Both camps were nervous, hence the extra men in the vicinity of the safe house.

Regardless of the intercamp rivalry, the Marchinskis would be desperate to protect their pawn. As long as they had Abby Mason, they were in a commanding position. Losing her, whether to a bunch of cops or to Dragomir Tsvetanov, was not something they would want.

Bolan didn't dwell too long on the whys of the situation. He was being pursued by a pair of enemy SUVs.

All he had were his weapons and his wits.

Plus an overwhelming desire to protect Abby Mason. He had freed her from her abductors. It was not in his nature to allow his success to be snatched away.

"Remember what I said earlier? About doing whatever I asked? No questions."

"Yes."

"In a little while, I'm going to tell you to jump out of the car and hide. I want you to stay hidden and not show yourself until I come back for you."

There was a brief silence. "O-kay."

"This is important, Abby. I need you to stay focused. There are cars following us. I need to deal with them."

"They're coming after me again?"

"Yes."

"Oh."

"Your dad told me you're pretty good at martial arts."

"Well, yes, but how's that going to help?"

"Right now, Abby, I want you out of this car."

"Why?"

"For what I have to do."

"I don't understand…" After a brief silence, Bolan knew she'd worked it out. "Oh. I understand now."

"When I give you the word, just go. Tuck and roll, take cover and stay there until I come and get you."

She didn't argue. The girl had enough sense not to question what he intended doing, because it would undoubtedly involve some kind of violent action, and he wouldn't want her close by. If he had to worry about her during some close action, it might distract him. The alternative, her being retaken by Marchinski's men, was not an acceptable option.

"Dad always said my martial arts training might come in handy one day," she said. "I never thought it would involve something like this."

Bolan stepped on the gas pedal, swinging the heavy SUV around a sharp bend in the narrow trail, dust clouding in their wake. His eyes scanned the route ahead. He checked the rearview mirror again and calculated that it had taken around five seconds for the chase cars to negotiate the bend.

"You ready for this, Abby?"

"Mr. Cooper, there's no other choice, is there?"

"Miss Mason, you guessed right."

Abby unclipped her seat belt, leaning across to grip the door handle.

"Just tell me when."

Bolan eased the SUV close to the side of the trail, feeling the tires bumping in the slight depression there. He held the wheel steady, fixing his gaze on the trail ahead. Dust still misted the rear view, kicked up by the SUV's wheels. It would help to mask what he was about to have the girl do.

The trail dipped, swung to the left, and Bolan took the SUV in a swift curve. The pursuing vehicles disappeared from view.

Bolan hit the brakes, lowering his speed as he saw a thick fall of foliage coming up. No close trees to present obstacles.

"Abby. Now!" he yelled.

The girl didn't question his command. She jerked on the door handle, pushed it open and went out. She hit the ground and executed a shoulder roll that threw her into the foliage. Her forward momentum took her through the greenery. Bolan leaned across and snatched at the door handle, pulling the door shut. When he looked in the rearview mirror Abby had vanished from sight....

ABBY FELT THE foliage envelop her. For a few seconds, everything was a blur of movement and noise. Dust from the departing SUV blew over where she had exited the car. She crashed deep into the greenery, her body jarred from the roll. Breath was driven from her as she landed. This was different from learning the moves on padded Tatami mats within the comfort of the dojo. Right now she had landed on hard earth and stones, with the tangled undergrowth as added discomfort.

She lay, winded, her senses jarred by the impact. As Abby tried to regain her breath, she heard the fading sound of Matt's vehicle, then the roar of the two pursuing SUVs as they raced by. And then it became quiet.

Abby lay where she was, feeling the ache of her bruised body. She moved her arms and legs. Nothing appeared broken. In fact, apart from the bruising, she seemed all right. After a minute she felt something warm running down her left cheek. She touched her face and felt blood trickling from a scratch. She rubbed it away. Abby sat up, then got on her hands and knees and moved back from the trail, deeper into the bushes. She kept moving until she was able to conceal herself fully. No one would be able to see her from the trail.

Now all she could do was wait until Matt Cooper came back for her....

21

The moment Abby vacated the SUV, Bolan stamped on the gas pedal and sent the car in a headlong rush down the dusty trail.

He gained enough distance to bring the SUV to a slithering stop as he took it around a wide bend in the trail. Bolan went EVA, moving to the rear of his vehicle. He tripped the catch on the tailgate door and swung it up. Reaching inside, Bolan grabbed the large canvas tote stored in the trunk. He yanked the heavy-duty zip open and reached inside the bag.

Mack Bolan followed the old adage *never take a knife to a gunfight.* And never knowing what he might end up facing, he made certain his ordnance would cover all eventualities.

As he turned away from the SUV, he had an M72 LAW in his hands and was already extending the tube, feeling the unit click into place as it locked and cocked. Bolan stepped to one side, clearing the SUV. He wasn't about to risk the backblast crippling his own vehicle.

The first pursuing SUV appeared, accelerating as it came around the bend. Bolan judged it to be around sixty feet away as he shouldered the LAW and found his target. The 66 mm projectile burst from the tube with a throaty sound, fins barely having time to extend as it covered the distance to the SUV. The HEAT warhead detonated as it went through the windshield, ripping the vehicle apart in an instant. The occupants were engulfed in the blast, bodies torn apart as the powerful explosion demolished the SUV. Flame and smoke gushed from the wreck and the SUV turned sideways, rolling for a few yards until it slammed against the thick trunk of a tree.

Bolan tossed the used LAW tube back inside the trunk, reaching for a preloaded H&K MP5. The 9 mm SMG had a 30-round magazine installed, the selector already on three-round bursts.

The second SUV had come to a jerky halt to avoid slamming into the burning vehicle, sliding on the dirt trail. Doors were thrust open before the car came to a full stop, armed figures moving into view. They skirted the wreck, one man raising an arm when he made out Bolan's moving figure through the smoke.

"Get that bastard…"

They were his final words.

Bolan cut loose with the MP5, catching the man mid-sentence. The double burst of 9 mm Parabellum slugs chopped his legs from under him and he went down screaming.

The second man of the trio fired but was forced to pause, fanning smoke from his eyes. Bolan turned the SMG on the shooter, hitting him with a triple burst that reduced his features to a bloody mask. The man fell, clutching at his face.

The survivor, seeing his partners fall, decided to surrender. He threw aside his firearm and called out to Bolan.

"No more," he rasped, coughing away smoke. "I quit. You got me."

Bolan's face was set as he took a couple of steps forward.

The hard guy dived to the ground, scrambling to draw a hideaway gun holstered on his ankle.

THE MP5 ROSE and spat out three more 9 mm slugs that ripped into the guy's chest and opened up his heart. The Marchinski man went down without another sound.

"Now I've got you," Bolan said quietly.

Then he delivered mercy rounds to the other two men.

Bolan returned to his SUV. He put his MP5 into the weapons bag, slammed the tailgate and climbed behind the wheel. Turning the vehicle around, he maneuvered past the Marchinski wheels. Behind him, black smoke rose into the open sky from the still-burning wreck.

He drove to the spot where Abby Mason had exited the SUV. Bolan stopped and eased out, his eyes picking out the broken foliage where she'd vanished in the greenery.

"Abby, time to go."

"What's the password?" he heard her muffled voice say.

Bolan failed to hold back a grin. "Mr. Cooper?"

The foliage crackled and swayed. Abby emerged looking disheveled and with a cut on one cheek.

"Are you all right?" she asked.

Bolan nodded. "What about you?"

"I should get my black belt after that roll."

"Yes, you should."

"Are there any more coming after us?"

"I hope not."

"I really would like to go home now."

She reached out and took one of Bolan's big hands in hers.

They walked back to the 4x4. Bolan got Abby inside and closed the door. He took out his cell and called Stony Man. Brognola picked up his call.

"Tell Mason I'm bringing his girl home."

"Anything else you need to tell me?"

Bolan gave him their location. "Send in local P.D. and a fire truck."

"Sounds bad."

"Only for the Marchinski crew I left behind."

Bolan climbed behind the wheel of the SUV. He passed the cell to Abby.

"Say hello to Uncle Hal."

While she spoke to her godfather, he placed the Desert Eagle, his holsters and knife in the small bag behind his seat. The Beretta went into the glove box where he could get at it quickly if it was needed.

"I hope Matt doesn't ask me to jump out of the car again. That was scary but fun, I guess."

"You made her jump out of the car?" Brognola queried when Bolan took the cell.

"The situation called for drastic action."

"Is she okay?"

"The way she's shaping up, you should recruit her in around ten years."

"I'm not sure her dad would approve."

Bolan signed off and put the cell away. He drove back to the main highway and turned the SUV toward the city.

A few minutes later, Bolan glanced at Abby and realized she had fallen asleep. He saw no reason to wake her. She'd been through a lot—a hell of a lot—but she was young, and given time and love, she would be able to put it behind her. He hoped that would happen.

Bolan thought about Larry Mason. With his daughter safe, the man could concentrate on making sure Leopold Marchinski stayed where he was. The mobster's plan had backfired, the threat was neutralized and Bolan was set to complete his takedown of the Marchinski and Tsvetanov organizations.

His upcoming strikes would reduce them both to tatters, hopefully destroying their power bases and scattering the survivors. But that would only begin once he had returned Abby Mason to her anxious father. That would be a moment to treasure.

22

Marchinski Residence

Bolan watched and waited, focusing on the Marchinski mansion. His whole being was centered on what lay ahead.

The Executioner was about to drive home the last nail in the Marchinski coffin. He was going to take down what was left of the organization in an Executioner hard strike.

There would be no kind of negotiation.

No sweetheart deals.

No surrender.

This was meat for the Executioner's grinder—taking down the dealers in death and misery, those who preyed on the weak. They had no respect for life. They poisoned and destroyed. If they had a god, it was money. To appease their greed, these men stole and manipulated.

If they were not removed from society, Marchinski and Tsvetanov would simply continue to plunder and corrupt.

There was no halfway solution. These criminals had placed themselves in his sights—and Mack Bolan was willing and able to pull the trigger, however many times it was needed.

When the news reached Leo Marchinski in his eight-by-eight cell, the mob boss would fully understand what zero tolerance meant. His epitaph would be written in the blood of his underlings....

THE SPRAWLING HOUSE stood in carefully tended grounds, which were surrounded by a stone wall. At the rear of the ten-bedroom, two-story building, a wide stone patio reached out to encompass a large swimming pool. Beyond that was a professional tennis court. Once the electronically controlled gates were opened, a long drive led from the road to the house and a paved semicircular parking area, which was large enough to accommodate at least a dozen cars.

Five expensive vehicles had been parked after delivering men from the Marchinski inner circle, who'd been gathered for a meeting by Lazlo Sabaroff.

With Gregor dead and Leo's hopes of escape ruined, Sabaroff had assumed control of the organization. This was the opportunity he'd been waiting for.

Sabaroff sat down behind Leo Marchinski's desk, allowing himself a smile as he sank into the soft, comfortable leather. He placed his hands flat on the polished surface, drumming his thick fingers, and gave a satisfied sigh.

Sabaroff sensed someone standing just outside the open door to Marchinski's office. He glanced up and recognized Keppler. The lawyer stepped inside, making a small gesture with his hands.

"It fits," he said.

"Close the door," Sabaroff replied.

Keppler obliged then crossed the expanse of thick carpet. He took the seat Sabaroff waved him into.

"Day one," Sabaroff said. "New management."

He watched Keppler's expression…saw him realize what Sabaroff meant.

"There's a great deal we need to discuss," Keppler said. "But personally, I believe the main concern is still the Tsvetanov problem. Once they become aware Leo isn't coming back…"

"They might very well step up their opposition," Sabaroff said. "Exactly what I've been thinking."

"So we have to decide which way to handle it. Do we hit them hard, or do we negotiate?"

Sabaroff leaned forward, a slow smile forming as he took in Keppler's suggestions.

"Leo would hit them with everything at his disposal. That was his way. The trouble is that would lead to prolonged war. We've had a bellyful of that already, and we've lost a number of good men. Add that to the mess at the safe house. Dead bodies all over, and we still don't know who snatched Mason's brat."

"There's been nothing from any of our contacts?"

"We can't find out a damn thing. If he's an undercover cop, he's really undercover. No one knows where he came from or where he's gone."

"Lazlo, don't shoot me when I say it, but the man was good."

Sabaroff waved a dismissal.

"Don't remind me. We need to look forward, to focus on how we keep this organization from falling apart." Sabaroff took a moment. "I still don't figure how he found out about the safe house."

Keppler steeled himself. He'd expected the question to come up. "The man was smart. He made all the right moves, Lazlo."

"Damn right," Sabaroff said. "So we need to move on."

"Seems you have that well in hand," Keppler said.

"Right now I have only one question. How do we handle Leo?"

"I'd have to say with everything that's just happened, we're going to find it hard to concentrate on his defense. Wouldn't you agree, counselor?"

Keppler's thin smile was instantaneous.

"We have no arguments left to offer," he said. "And now the girl has been freed so Mason has no reason to acquiesce to our demands."

"Well, my friend, it seems we're at a stalemate. Leo will have to take his chances with the law."

"That would be my advice."

"Which I accept."

Sabaroff rose to his feet and crossed to the wet bar, where he poured two generous whiskies. He handed one to Keppler. They drank in satisfied silence.

"As legal counsel for the organization," Sabaroff said, "you should be present for this meeting."

"Of course. Whatever you need, Mr. Sabaroff."

Sabaroff picked up the internal phone.

"Bring them in, Petre."

WHEN THE DOOR was opened and the six men were ushered into the office, Sabaroff had resumed his seat behind the desk, with Keppler at his side.

"Sit down," Sabaroff said.

He waited until the group was seated. The man who had escorted them in, Petre, stood to one side until Sabaroff caught his eye.

"Would you get everyone a drink, Petre?"

While this was being arranged, Sabaroff faced his audience.

"By now we all know what has happened. The safe house was attacked. Gregor was killed and the girl we were holding has been removed from our care. Which means the arrangement we were negotiating with Mason has been closed. Leo will not receive his get-out-of-jail-free pass. I have discussed this with Mr. Keppler, and unless divine intervention occurs, Leo is going to be found guilty. As his second in command, I have stepped in, and I now take control." Sabaroff paused for his pronouncement to be absorbed by the group. "If anyone would like to challenge my decision, by all means speak up. We are, after all, in America—the land of free speech and democracy."

A faint, almost subliminal murmur sounded. Quick glances flashed between the men, and some of them shuffled their feet. While this was taking place, Petre was moving around the room, passing out glasses of expensive whiskey.

"Lazlo—Mr. Sabaroff—is better placed to lead than anyone in this room," Keppler said quickly. "He has been SIC for a long time. He understands the complexities of running an organization like ours. We can't forget that he has been responsible for handling most of the day-to-day business. Right now we need to stand together against the Tsvetanov threat. We must also be able to fulfill current contracts and keep our operations running smoothly."

"It's that or go bust," Sabaroff said. "Anything we allow to slide, the Tsvetanovs will snatch away. We don't let that happen."

"What if they don't back away?" one of the men asked.

"We make them." Sabaroff smiled. "You haven't forgotten how to do that, have you?"

That brought a brief rumble of approval—even a little nervous laughter.

"We stay focused," Sabaroff said. "We keep the ball rolling. If we do that, there are still good days ahead. Days we can all profit by."

The final statement drew them in. Watching the men, Sabaroff smiled briefly. He had them in his grasp now. It was going to be okay.

23

From the first day of his War Everlasting, Mack Bolan
had set his rules. No mercy for the unjust. Those who
had no mercy for the innocent would not receive any
from Bolan.

As he crouched in the early-evening shadows, the
trees that bordered the property behind him, Bolan
watched the house and assessed his moves. He had
already counted at least four guards patrolling the
grounds and watching for unwelcome visitors. The attack on the safe house had proved to them they were
far from safe. So these moving targets would be ready
and waiting.

He wore the holstered Beretta 93R and Desert Eagle.
A knife was strapped to his thigh and a 9 mm Uzi hung
from a neck strap. Bolan cradled an MP5 in his hands.
His combat harness held additional magazines for each
weapon. Slung across his back was an M32 MGL. The
Milkor Multiple Grenade Launcher carried a six-load
cylinder that could take 40 mm grenades in various
categories; Bolan had two M406 HE loads, followed
by M680 Smoke, and a final pair of M576 buckshot
rounds. He also carried a number of thermite grenades
in his combat harness.

The two front sentries started to talk, their attention

slackening. Bolan eased forward to give himself a clear area. He raised the M32 and calculated the distance to the grouped vehicles.

Bolan tripped the trigger, sending the first HE grenade on its arc. He shifted the launcher and fired the second M406 high-explosive round.

The dull thump of the grenades landing was followed by a burst of flame and smoke. The targets were rocked by the blasts, the expanding fireballs hitting the vehicles close by. Fuel tanks burst and spilled flaming gasoline. The detonations galvanized the sentries into a reaction.

By this time, Bolan had the grenade launcher dangling by its strap as he brought the Uzi into play, stepping out of the gloom. His opening bursts caught the pair of sentries as they pulled out their own SMGs. They were too late. Bolan hit them hard and with an accuracy they could never have matched. As the 9 mm slugs ripped into their bodies, the pair was knocked off their feet, unfired weapons slipping from loose fingers. The pair was still falling when a third shooter appeared from the side of the house. He lost precious seconds as he took in the blazing, wrecked cars and two of his buddies down on the ground.

Those seconds were his last as Bolan tracked in with the Uzi and hit him with a burst. The slugs shattered his ribs as they cut into his body and punched through to his heart and lungs. The man crumpled without a sound, facedown on the hard ground.

Bolan had been moving forward as he triggered the burst, and now he let the Uzi dangle as he switched back to the MGL. He aimed at the main window fronting the house and laid down an M680 smoke grenade. It smashed through the glass and dropped inside. Bolan moved across the frontage, going for the other main window and repeating the action. As the second window shattered, thick white smoke was already expanding through the first room.

Swinging the MGL out of the way, Bolan raised the Uzi again as he made for the house. He picked up movement off his left and saw the fourth outside sentry moving to intercept. The man opened up with his SMG. Bolan paused in midstride and unleashed a long burst from the Uzi. His shots hit the sentry midthigh. The man grunted and folded at the knees, dropping into the path of Bolan's follow-up shots. They slammed into his upper chest and clipped his throat. The guy went down with a fountain of blood erupting from his torn throat.

Turning back toward the house, Bolan saw the front doors swing inward. Some thin tendrils of smoke whipped out, briefly curling around the pair of armed figures rushing from the entrance. Bolan dropped to one knee and hauled the M32 launcher into play. He fired the first of his M576 buckshot rounds at the pair. The short range kept the spread close, but the shot found targets in both men moving at Bolan. Twenty #4 shot pellets hit the men hard, tearing at them with brutal force. They fell as Bolan walked by them into the entrance hall. He left them lying in their own blood and viscera.

Smoke was coming through the doors on Bolan's left and right. A wide staircase lay straight ahead. Bolan heard yelling voices interspersed by choking coughs. He moved toward the doors and crouched with his back against the closest wall.

He pushed out the empty shell casing from the M32 and reloaded, then he pulled out a couple of thermite grenades. He pulled the first pin and lobbed the canister onto the upper landing. Bolan tossed the second grenade along the passage, toward the rear of the house.

A door crashed open, and coughing figures stumbled into the hall, bringing white smoke with them. Despite being barely able to see, their eyes reddened and streaming tears, every man carried a weapon.

Except one.

Stumbling in the smoke, his usually cool demeanor lost in the frantic flight, Jason Keppler was jostled and pushed by the others. His legal brain gave him no comfort right now. Whatever trickery he employed within the hushed confines of the courtroom meant nothing here. He was just another member of the Marchinski mob, a high-priced mouthpiece who minutes earlier had been congratulating himself on maneuvering his own career in a new direction.

His future prospects faded into the background amid the yelling and general confusion, and Jason Keppler became just another criminal about to fall at the hands of Mack Bolan, the Executioner.

Bolan turned the M32 in their direction and pumped off two shots. The buckshot pellets shredded expensive suits and vulnerable flesh. The men tumbled back, yelling, screaming, their blood spattering the wall and door.

The opposite door was wrenched open. Three gasping members of the Marchinski organization blundered into view, thick smoke crowding behind them. Bolan swung the grenade launcher around and triggered one of his two remaining buckshot rounds at targets no more than six feet from where he crouched.

In an explosion of blood, torn flesh and shredded clothing, the men were knocked sideways, torn limbs unable to hold them upright any longer.

Even in the blur of the moment, Bolan recognized the last man out of the room.

Lazlo Sabaroff, Leo Marchinski's SIC. The man

clutched an auto pistol in his hand, rubbing tears from his eyes with the sleeve of his expensive suit.

"Son of a bitch," Sabaroff screamed when he spotted Bolan's black-clad form. "You think this will end here? Dragomir is wrong…"

He put out his gun arm, finger pulling back on the trigger.

Bolan's MGL fired first, spitting out a lethal load of buckshot that caught Sabaroff in the gut, the concentrated, short-range spread tearing him open and almost severing his torso in half. Sabaroff dropped, mouth gaping in a pain-filled moment that rendered him silent.

At the head of the wide staircase the thermite canister had erupted, the contents creating an incandescent blaze that was spreading along the timber floor and into the rooms on the second floor. The second thermite grenade was already spreading its powerful and hungry burn down the passage. The high percentage of wood in the house's construction would feed the fire as it spread through the building.

Bolan heard a sudden dull thump as one of the stricken cars out front gave up its fuel tank. Seconds later, another tank blew.

Bolan slung the MGL across his back again and switched to the MP5 as he made for the exit. When he stepped through the front door, he saw that the parked cars were still engulfed in heavy flame. Burning gasoline had been thrown in a wide arc from the burst tanks. Paintwork was blistering and cracking. Tires bubbled and threw out dense black smoke. Bolan heard window glass splintering under the high temperature. The whole area was taking on the appearance of a war zone.

Bolan turned away and headed back to his ingress point and the SUV he'd left a half mile back.

As Bolan cleared the end of the house, flames starting to glow behind the upstairs windows, movement caught his attention. He brought the MP5 on line as he made out a figure struggling from one of the ground-level side windows. The man dropped heavily to the ground, frantically slapping at his smoldering clothing. Even his hair was smoking from the heat he'd just escaped. He struggled out of his scorching jacket, throwing it aside, and his head half turned. He came face-to-face with Bolan and took in the heavily armed, black-clad figure. He made the connection, cursing loudly. His right hand snatched at the big auto pistol in the shoulder rig he was wearing, yanking the weapon free and swinging the muzzle at Bolan.

The MP5 crackled briefly, the burn of 9 mm slugs causing the man to gasp as he fell back against the side of the house, letting go of his pistol as he slid to the ground.

Bolan didn't hesitate before moving on. He never took pleasure in staring at the dead. He did what he needed to do and walked away.

Behind him, the Marchinski house burned with a growing fury—a cleansing flame that would bring the building to the ground and leave nothing but a pile of ashes.

The trees and bushes closed around Bolan as he tramped through them. He retraced his unhurried steps until he finally reached the Suburban. Taking the remote from a side pocket, he unlocked the tailgate. Bolan removed his weapons and placed them inside the bag resting on the trunk floor. Then he quickly peeled off the blacksuit and replaced it with civilian clothing. Light gray slacks and a white shirt. He slipped into a leather jacket and closed the tailgate. He had retained the 93R and placed it in the glove box once he was behind the wheel.

Bolan fired up the powerful motor, eased into gear and reversed the big SUV. He followed a narrow trail that would allow him to rejoin the highway after a few miles.

Once he had an opening, Bolan rolled onto the tarmac, turning in the direction of the city. He flicked on his lights, settling into a steady speed. In the first couple of miles, he saw no other traffic.

When he glanced into the rearview mirror, he made out the orange shading of the sky from the distant fire.

The police and fire department would be called to the scene very soon, but by then he would be well clear of the area.

It had been a successful operation—in and out with the minimum of distractions.

Engagement.

Dispersal.

Retreat.

A Bolan Blitz.

BOLAN PARKED UP at a truck stop and made his call to Stony Man. Hal Brognola picked up.

"Been waiting for your call," the big Fed said. "Mission accomplished?"

"Half of it," Bolan replied. "I'm on my way to tie the rest down."

"How're you doing, pal?"

"I'll be glad when this is over."

"Busy few days?"

"You could say."

"Your new best friend is back home. Thought I'd let you know."

Bolan managed a weary smile at that news.

"Makes it all worthwhile, then. She's a remarkable young lady."

"Striker, all she could talk about was her feat of jumping out of a moving car and hiding in the bushes."

"And Larry?"

"He said to tell you he wants to shake your hand until your arm drops off. You did what you promised, Striker. Larry will never forget it."

"Glad to be of help."

"One more thing he told me. He can't wait to visit Leo Marchinski and let him know there's no way he'll be walking out of jail. It'll be the icing on the cake." There was a brief pause. "You've got my thanks, too, Striker. That little girl is special to me. I won't forget what you've done."

"No problem. Is there any update on the Tsvetanov crew?"

"Nothing we can add. You know as much about them as we do. They don't appear to have a redeeming quality about them."

"I'll tell them what you said when I meet them."

"You come home safe, Striker."

Bolan shut down the call. He guided the SUV across the parking lot and onto the highway. When he checked the sat-nav display, Bolan saw it would take him directly to the Tsvetanov home base and another killing ground.

24

Lexi Bulin found Tsvetanov in the main office of the warehouse complex. Bulin had a look on his face that told the crime boss this was not an interruption he was going to enjoy.

"You'll want to hear this," Bulin said.

"If it's about the Marchinskis, I doubt it. Those bastards have done enough to us over the past few days."

"I just had word that the Marchinski organization has been blown apart. Somebody hit a safe house and killed Gregor Marchinski. Then Marchinski's house was burned to the ground. Most of his top guys are dead—including Sabaroff."

"Who did this? I'd like to give him a medal."

"You might not when I tell you what I'm thinking."

Tsvetanov put down the stack of bills he'd been checking.

"No games, Lexi. What's on your mind?"

"This started when we were hit earlier. Then the Marchinskis took a loss. We figured they hit us, and they must have thought we hit them. Now somebody snatched the kid the Marchinskis kidnapped. That definitely didn't come from us. It's all too convenient, like it's been staged to cause a war between us and the Marchinskis."

"And we didn't take down the Marchinski house," Tsvetanov admitted. "So who the hell is stirring the pot?"

"None of these hits shouts cops. Much as they'd like to, police don't come on like a squad of Rambo clones."

"So what do we have? Some guy playing vigilante?"

"If he is, the mother has one hell of an arsenal."

"Have you spoken to our sources?"

Bulin nodded. "Nothing. There are no hints of covert ops from any department."

"So we're looking at a fresh player trying to clear the way for a new organization?" Tsvetanov slammed his fist against the desktop. "*Svoloch.* We find him. I want him here so I can cut him into little pieces."

Tsvetanov slammed his clenched fist down again.

The thud was followed by a sudden, distant crackle of auto fire. Angry voices called out in alarm.

"What the hell is that?" Tsvetanov yelled.

"I have a feeling we have a visitor…" Bulin said. "Uninvited."

THE SAT NAV had led Bolan directly to the warehouse compound. It stood behind a rusting steel fence with weeds sprouting between the cracks in the concrete apron. A trio of new vehicles was parked in front of a line of gray uninspiring buildings.

The rain slanting out of the dark sky only added to the depressing isolation of the area.

A man lounged against the side of one black 4x4. He glanced up when Bolan's Suburban sped in through the open entrance, headlights blazing.

Bolan's mood allowed for no compromise. With the

Marchinski organization in tatters, he wanted an end to the whole affair.

The man snatched an auto pistol from his belt and opened fire. Only one bullet found a target, the slug clipping the edge of the Chevy's roof.

Bolan planted his foot down on the gas pedal, sending the big vehicle in a short curve. The shooter tried to step back, but he was too slow. The front of the speeding vehicle lifted him off his feet, spinning him over the hood. The thump of the hard impact was lost in the roar of the engine. The man's body was tossed in the air, turning over and over before it hit the concrete. He slammed down hard, one leg twisted beneath his body as bone snapped. Blood pooled beneath his shattered skull.

Jamming on the brakes, Bolan brought the Suburban to a rubber-scorching halt, shoving open his door and exiting the rocking vehicle. He wore his blacksuit again, with a combat harness in place. He carried his Desert Eagle on his right hip, the Beretta in his shoulder rig and he was wielding a fully loaded MP5. The 30-round magazine had a second unit taped in place, providing an additional 30-round capacity.

He went directly to the wooden access door, slamming a booted foot against the weathered wood. The door crashed in, and Bolan breached the entrance, going in fast and swerving to one side as he entered the warehouse.

The interior was deep and wide, the floor space heavily stacked with goods. The piled cartons vied for space with a number of brand-new, expensive cars and SUVs; the vehicles were still in factory condition, with protective tapes on windows and headlamps; none of them had any license plates.

Bolan took a spot behind a gleaming Cadillac, his eyes scanning the interior of the warehouse. He spotted movement near the partitioned office section to his right. Raised voices echoed through the building.

A pair of armed figures appeared from behind high stacks of cartons. They were moving in Bolan's general direction.

The Executioner had no intention of allowing them to get close. He leaned out from his crouching position, the muzzle of the MP5 tracking the movement of the two shooters.

He dropped the closest man with a short burst from the H&K, and the shooter went down with a harsh screech, flopping around on the concrete floor. His partner opened fire on Bolan's position, a prolonged burst of auto fire that punched ragged holes through the expensive bodywork of the Cadillac, instantly lowering its market value.

Bolan stayed low, swinging his MP5 to follow the man's advance. He fired off a long burst that hammered at the shooter's midsection. The man went up on his toes, the SMG in his hands sending slugs at the roofline. His torn body stiffened, and he toppled heavily on his back, kicking at the concrete floor.

Farther in the building, Bolan picked up the sound of agitated voices. He caught a glimpse of moving figures, bobbing back and forth in the shadows. Bolan plucked a fragmentation grenade from his harness, drew the pin and lobbed the projectile over the roofs of the parked vehicles. It exploded with an echoing thump. Men screamed as they were riddled by metal fragments. One man was lifted off his feet and bounced off the side of a car. Bolan took two more grenades and deployed them. One skittered across the floor and slid beneath one of the parked SUVs, the explosion lifting the heavy car off the floor, the blast puncturing the fuel tank. An oily ball of flame rolled across the area. Bolan heard the second grenade burn. The concussion shattered vehicle windows and ripped open the expensive bodywork. Following the final explosion, a second fuel tank blew, throwing fiery tendrils across the parked vehicles. The whole building was going to burn down.

LEXI BULIN DREW his 9 mm SIG. Even as he closed his fingers around the grips, he could feel his sweat, greasy against the plastic.

The auto fire echoing around the warehouse made him feel sick. Flames from the demolished cars were spreading across the building, reaching the roof in some areas. Smoke was starting to build up. This was a situation he had never been in before. He was an organizer, not a shooter; the closest he came to using a gun was on the firing range.

He glanced across at Tsvetanov. The man had a shotgun in his hands and was racking a shell into the breach.

"He wants to take me on, I'm ready. No asshole gets the better of Drago Tsvetanov in his own house."

He kicked a chair out of his way and crossed the office, yanking the door wide and bracing himself in the opening.

"Show yourself!"

THE BLACK-CLAD FIGURE appeared out of the gloom, backlit by the blaze consuming the building. He was moving fast so that Tsvetanov had no chance to set him in his sights. All Tsvetanov saw was the dull gleam of the man's weapon. That view lasted for no more than a couple of seconds.

The SMG fired, a prolonged burst that flickered with flame from the muzzle. Drago Tsvetanov felt the solid impact of the 9 mm slugs as they tore into him. He felt no initial pain, only the driving force that pushed him back against the office door. Glass shattered. Tsvetanov hung there for a few seconds then slid to a sitting position. The pain hit him then, his body leaking blood from the multiple wounds. He choked on blood, slipping forward until his curled body lay facedown on the cold floor.

As BOLAN STEPPED FORWARD, he caught movement inside the office as Lexi Bulin edged toward the exit, still carrying the SIG. He had to have seen what happened to Tsvetanov.

The sight of the black-clad figure, favoring an MP5, was enough to dissuade Lexi Bulin from doing anything foolish.

He stepped over Tsvetanov's bloody corpse and held his pistol in a nonaggressive position.

"I quit," he said. "I'm done…"

"Tell me something I don't know," Bolan replied.

Bulin narrowed his eyes, and his hand tightened its grip on the SIG.

THE H&K CRACKLED. Bulin's body erupted in a series of bloody holes as the long burst shredded his torso. He fell back over Tsvetanov's body, halfway inside the office.

Bolan walked away, pausing briefly to activate a thermite grenade on the closest stack of contraband goods. The fiery hunger from the relentless chemical reaction would make certain nothing was left of the illicit goods. He slipped out through the door and climbed into his SUV. Bolan swung the vehicle around and drove out of the compound. As he turned onto the service road, flames were already starting to show behind the streaked glass of the warehouse.

Before he made the highway, Bolan parked to remove his assault gear and pull on a plain topcoat. With his weapons stored in the carry bag, Bolan pulled away and picked up the route that would take him to his motel.

His mission was complete.

The Marchinski and Tsvetanov mobs were out of business.

Leo Marchinski would soon be receiving the news that his get-out-of-jail-free ticket had been canceled.

Larry Mason would enjoy delivering that message. Not as much as he would enjoy arriving home to find that his daughter had been returned safe and well.

Epilogue

The media had called the events between the Marchin-ski and Tsvetanov organizations an internecine clash. No one was about to correct that statement—especially not Mack Bolan or Stony Man.

Since the conclusion of Bolan's involvement, there had been a major scuffle to reorganize from both sides. In the end, little came of it. Too much internal damage had been done. As a result of the takedown, police and FBI had concentrated on the survivors, pulling a number of them off the streets in various locations. Coupled with information retrieved from the former main residences, names came to light, revealing sources feeding the organizations. There were some surprises when these names were revealed. Arrests followed, confessions began and bargains were demanded.

The bodies of Nancy Cleland and Harry Jigs were finally laid to rest.

For Bolan and Brognola, the highlight was the return of Abby Mason to her father.

A brief meeting was arranged between Bolan and the Masons. Brognola showed up, as well.

Abby, back in the safety of her home, showed little trauma from her ordeal. She had hugged Brognola and then turned to Bolan.

"I've been practicing my shoulder rolls," she announced.

"Why's that?" Bolan asked.

"Because when I grow up, I want to be just like you—one of the good guys."

Those few words, delivered with childlike solemnity, advised Mack Bolan that he was still on the side of the angels.

* * * * *

The Executioner®
Don Pendleton's
MAXIMUM CHAOS

The mob will stop at nothing to free a ruthless killer

Desperate to escape conviction, the head of a powerful mob orders the kidnapping of a federal prosecutor's daughter. If the mobster isn't freed, if anyone contacts the authorities, the girl will be killed. Backed into a corner, her father must rely on the one man who can help: Mack Bolan.

Finding the girl won't be easy. Plus, with an innocent life at stake, going in guns blazing is a risk Bolan can't take. His only choice is to pit the crime syndicate against their rivals. The mob is about to get a visit from the Executioner. And this time he's handing out death penalties.

Available October wherever books and ebooks are sold.

GOLD EAGLE®

GEX431

Don Pendleton
DEATH DEALERS

A deadly weapons auction turns Hawaii into a terrorist destination

Terrorists from around the world have gathered in Hawaii to bid on stolen missiles. Whoever wins will have a weapon powerful enough to destroy an aircraft carrier with a single shot. With the clock ticking, Able Team goes undercover to stop the auction and take down the arms dealer who set up the buy. Meanwhile, Phoenix Force is on the hunt to retrieve the missiles and do whatever is necessary to eliminate the shadowy group behind the theft.

STONY MAN®

Available December wherever books and ebooks are sold.

Or order your copy now by sending your name, address, zip or postal code, along with a check or money order (please do not send cash) for $6.99 for each book ordered ($7.99 in Canada), plus 75¢ postage and handling ($1.00 in Canada), payable to Gold Eagle Books, to:

In the U.S.	**In Canada**
Gold Eagle Books	Gold Eagle Books
3010 Walden Avenue	P.O. Box 636
P.O. Box 9077	Fort Erie, Ontario
Buffalo, NY 14269-9077	L2A 5X3

Please specify book title with your order.
Canadian residents add applicable federal and provincial taxes.

GOLD EAGLE®

Don Pendleton's Mack Bolan

CHAIN REACTION

An old adversary's illicit plot threatens global security...

When a Stony Man Farm nemesis is suspected in the death of two FBI agents, Mack Bolan gets called into action. The last time Bolan crossed paths with the shadowy criminal organization, he annihilated their operations in North Korea. Now the group has brokered a deal that would send weapons-grade uranium to Iran in exchange for a cache of stolen diamonds. Joining forces with a field operative, Bolan sets off on a shattering cross-continental firefight. Bolan has no choice: he must destroy the criminal conspiracy behind the threat. Once and for all.

Available October wherever books and ebooks are sold.

Or order your copy now by sending your name, address, zip or postal code, along with a check or money order (please do not send cash) for $6.99 for each book ordered ($7.99 in Canada), plus 75¢ postage and handling ($1.00 in Canada), payable to Gold Eagle Books, to:

In the U.S.
Gold Eagle Books
3010 Walden Avenue
P.O. Box 9077
Buffalo, NY 14269-9077

In Canada
Gold Eagle Books
P.O. Box 636
Fort Erie, Ontario
L2A 5X3

Please specify book title with your order.
Canadian residents add applicable federal and provincial taxes.

GOLD EAGLE®

Don Pendleton's Mack Bolan

NIGHTMARE ARMY

A wealthy industrialist plots the ultimate ethnic cleansing...

Attacked by feral, rampaging villagers infected by a synthetic virus, Mack Bolan barely escapes. Determined to find the source of this powerful bioweapon, Bolan tracks the virus to a secret facility, where scientists are working to make the infected victims stronger, swifter and more deadly. But the wealthy industrialist funding this research has his sights set on all-out toxic warfare.

With the germ ready, it will be unleashed across the European Union, targeting specific ethnic groups for destruction. With millions of lives at stake, Bolan has no choice but to embark on a seek-and-destroy mission.

Available December wherever books and ebooks are sold.

Or order your copy now by sending your name, address, zip or postal code, along with a check or money order (please do not send cash) for $6.99 for each book ordered ($7.99 in Canada), plus 75¢ postage and handling ($1.00 in Canada), payable to Gold Eagle Books, to:

In the U.S.	**In Canada**
Gold Eagle Books	Gold Eagle Books
3010 Walden Avenue	P.O. Box 636
P.O. Box 9077	Fort Erie, Ontario
Buffalo, NY 14269-9077	L2A 5X3

Please specify book title with your order.
Canadian residents add applicable federal and provincial taxes.

GOLD EAGLE

GSB170